RAY COMFORT

THE MYSTERY

A TALE OF TWO WARS

genesis
PUBLISHING GROUP

The Mystery: A Tale of Two Wars

Published by
Genesis Publishing Group
2002 Skyline Place
Bartlesville, OK 74006
www.genesis-group.net

Edited by Lynn Copeland

Cover illustration by Erik Hollander, erikhollanderdesign.com

Cover layout, page design, and production by Genesis Group

ISBN 978-1-933591-17-9 (pbk.)
ISBN 978-1-933591-18-6 (e-book)

Printed in the United States of America

CHARACTERS

❦

Jeremiah (Jerry) P. Adamson—lead character
Samuel Adamson—Jerry's father
Esther Adamson—Jerry's mother
Lillian Adamson—Jerry's sister
Hilda—Samuel's mother
Karl von Ludendorff—Jerry's childhood friend
Mr. von Ludendorff—Karl's father
Joseph Greenberg—Samuel's cousin
Marian—French Resistance member
Jean Moulin—French Resistance leader
Henri—French Resistance member
Andre—French Resistance member
Rachel—Jewish woman
Rabbi Cohen—Jewish rabbi
Charles—French Resistance member
Francois Berdau—French Resistance member
Ingrid Berdau—Francois's wife
Pierre—French Resistance member
Jacques—French Resistance member
Connie—Jerry's wife
Johnny—Jerry's son
Elizabeth—Jerry's daughter
Bill Lovock—Farm worker

The Mystery

Vance—Jerry's accountant
Theodore and Grace Lawson—Jerry's neighbors
Darlene—Johnny's girlfriend
Jack—Dallas nightclub owner
Lips—Drug dealer
Edwin Smalley—Connie's minister

Contents

~~~

CHAPTER ONE
ENEMIES OF THE STATE

∞◦∞

J ERRY COULD feel his heart pounding like a hammer in his chest. Blood gushed from his left shoulder as he rounded the corner of what was once a bakery in the city of Bialystok, Poland. Many times he had casually walked to the bakery with friends, purchased soft white bread and eaten it while it was still hot. But bread was the last thing on his mind as he fled for his life like a wounded animal, pursued by three Nazi soldiers.

Minutes earlier, he and his beloved father had run out the back door as the soldiers burst through the front of their home. Shots rang out, one hitting his father and another striking Jerry in the shoulder. His father dropped to his knees and with an impassioned cry, yelled, "Run, Jerry! *Run!*"

As he rounded the corner, he remembered the narrow alley between the bakery and a shoe store. At the end of the alley stood about two dozen old wooden crates piled against a six-foot fence. On one side of the crates was a 14-inch-high gap into which he often crawled. That opening led to a crawlspace underneath the bakery, a cramped but suitable hideout for smoking cigarettes with another teenage friend, something his father would have frowned upon ... if he knew.

Jerry's eyes were wild with terror, not only because he had been shot and was being chased by Nazis, but for fear of what had happened to his father. As he crawled under the bakery floor he heard another two shots ring out. He stopped moving and whispered, "Dear God ... what is happening?"

The ground was damp and cold and there was barely room for him to lift his head. He tried to inspect his bleeding shoulder. It appeared to be just a flesh wound but it scared him. The bullet had entered at the back of his shoulder, missed the bone and passed through the front, tearing the flesh as it went. It was burning as though it had been clamped in a red-hot steel vise, causing uncontrollable groans to well up from within him. His breathing was deep and fast and his chest heaved and burned as the chilled night air was drawn into his lungs. He clenched his teeth and closed his eyes to try to stop the tears, both from the pain of his shoulder and the dread that gripped his heart. Even with his right hand held tightly over the injury, his sleeve was crimson with blood down to his wrist.

His eyes widened in fear at the thought that entered his mind. *What if he had left a trail of blood?* Suddenly he heard footsteps! It was the unmistakable sound of leather-soled boots crunching the stones in the alley. Jerry held his blood-drenched hand over his mouth to quiet his loud breathing. He could hear voices, and through the cracks of the wooden foundation he could see the legs of the three soldiers who had terrorized his family. *His mother and sister!* What had happened to them, and to his grandmother, back at the house? He prayed that the soldiers had left them alone. As far as he knew, it was only the men who were being rounded up and shot.

From the German dialect he had learned, Jerry heard one of the soldiers say, "He's just a lad!" Then he said something Jerry couldn't understand. The footsteps then headed off into the distance, followed by silence.

Jerry slowly removed his hand from his mouth, took a deep blood-tasting breath, and gave a guarded sigh of relief. With daylight beginning to dawn, it would be twelve long hours before he dared to move, and in the safety of nightfall make his way back to his home.

WHAT WAS AN American family doing in Bialystok, Poland, in 1939? Six years earlier, Samuel Adamson sat on his farm porch in Texas, reading the newspaper. Samuel sure looked like a farmer. He was a wiry-framed five foot ten with a weathered body that showed signs of the outdoors. The hot southern sun had left him tanned with an earthy appearance, as he leaned forward with interest in what he was reading. His pipe sat as stationary in his mouth as he did in his old wooden chair. It was September 1933. On the home-front Robert A. Chesebrough, the chemist who invented Vaseline, had died. The ninety-six-year-old attributed his long life to eating a spoonful of the sticky substance each day. Samuel raised an eyebrow and mumbled, "Probably choked to death."

Overseas, the largest political group in Germany, Adolf Hitler's Nazi Party, had enacted a controversial program of involuntary sterilization. The program was for people who were said to be "idiots" or schizophrenics, suffer from depression or epilepsy, or have physical weaknesses like deafness or blindness. Samuel had followed the political life of Hitler since the early twenties. Not that he sought out what the man was doing, but simply because whatever he did was news. Hitler had joined the German Workers' Party in 1919 at age thirty, and the very first time he spoke his hearers were impressed with his oratory skills. In later recounting the experience in *Mein Kampf* Hitler wrote: "I spoke for thirty minutes, and what before I had simply felt within me, without in any way knowing it, was now proved by reality: I could speak! After thirty minutes the people in the small room were electrified and the enthusiasm was first expressed by the fact that my appeal to the self-sacrifice of those present led to the donation of three hundred marks."

Pleased with his verbal prowess, the German Workers' Party began promoting Hitler as their main attraction. He spoke passionately against the Treaty of Versailles with anti-Semitic outbursts, blaming the Jews for almost all of Germany's problems. Many empathized with his message and joined the Party.

In February 1920, the German Workers' Party began to hold its first mass meetings, with Hitler outlining its political platform. These Twenty Five Points of the German Workers' Party included: the union of all Germans in a greater German Reich; rejection of the binding Versailles Treaty; the demand for additional territories for the German people (*Lebensraum*); citizenship determined by race with no Jew to be considered a German; the confiscation of all income not earned by work; a thorough reconstruction of the national education system; religious freedom, except for religions which endanger the German race; and a strong central government for the execution of effective legislation.

As he read through the Twenty Five Points, Hitler asked the rowdy crowd for its approval on each one. And they certainly approved. "When after nearly four hours the hall began to empty and the crowd, shoulder to shoulder, began to move, shove, press toward the exit like a slow stream," Hitler recounted, "I knew that now the principles of a movement which could no longer be forgotten were moving out among the German people…A fire was kindled from whose flame one day the sword must come which would regain freedom for the Germanic Siegfried and life for the German nation."

Not long after that Hitler chose the symbol of his fledgling movement: the swastika, a symbol Samuel had seen often as the American press reported on this man's rising popularity. "In the red we see the social idea of the movement," Hitler explained, "in the white the national idea, in the swastika the mission to struggle for the victory of Aryan man and at the same time the victory of the idea of creative work, which is eternally anti-Semitic and will always be anti-Semitic."

But it wasn't until 1933 that Samuel became concerned about Adolf Hitler and his political aspirations. Samuel's mother was a German Jew living in Waldenberg, and even though many spoke of Hitler with a new sense of excitement, with each passing day he grew increasingly uneasy about the policies of the Nazi Party. In April of that year, Jews in Germany were officially prohibited from holding public office or civil service positions and were prevented from involvement in the legal field. Two weeks later, Samuel read where Jewish students were affected by the "Law against Overcrowding in Schools and Universities." Then, on July 14, the De-Naturalization Law allowed the Third Reich to remove the citizenship of Jews and other "undesirables."

With his mother being Jewish, Samuel wished he could be nearer so he could keep an eye out for her. That was one of the reasons Samuel Adamson decided to leave his beloved farm in the hands of a trustworthy friend and move his small family to Germany.

Although their farm had been doing quite well, the 1929 stock market crash had a devastating effect on the U.S. As what was being called the Great Depression deepened its hold, unemployment increased to an all-time high. Throughout the country, it was common to see long lines outside rescue missions, as hungry people waited to get food for their families.

When the Adamsons's farming market ground to a halt, it seemed a good time to start over somewhere else. They had just enough money to pay for the long boat trip and set up some sort of business.

After the death of Samuel's father, his mother had carried on the family clothing store, building up a number of regular customers over the years—and her business was going reasonably well until recently. But the Nazis had begun posting billboards all over the country saying "German people, defend yourselves! Do not buy from Jews!" They publicly burned books that were considered "un-German," and were revising the school curriculum to teach "race science." According to Wilhelm Frick, the Nazi Interior Minister, "The schools must constantly emphasize that the infiltration of the German people with alien blood, especially Jewish and Negro, must be prevented."

Unsure of exactly what they were getting themselves into, on a cold January day in 1934, Samuel and his wife, Esther, sailed from New York with their two children. Lillian, age twelve, had been named after the popular actress Lillian Gish. When her parents were first married they saw the star in Victor Seastrom's MGM film *The Wind*, and she left such an impression on them that they decided to name their first girl after her.

Two years younger, Jeremiah was named after the biblical prophet, at the insistence of his Jewish grandmother. He hated the name and was pleased that his friends called him Jerry. As he grew older he came to prefer the seasoned sound of "Jeremiah," but even though he always introduced himself that way, people consistently reverted to "Jerry."

After a long voyage across the Atlantic on the French liner *Normandie*, the family arrived on the shores of France, then traveled by train to Waldenberg, Germany.

Samuel and Esther immediately sensed a climate of fear in the city, as people hurried about and kept to themselves. Nazis were everywhere, with their neatly fitted uniforms and their rigid manner, constantly stopping people to check their documentation.

Samuel's mother, Hilda, was standing anxiously at the back of the railway station's platform, waiting for soldiers to inspect the family's credentials. Her clothes were plain and colorless, and as she stood clutching her bag with her scarf pulled tightly around her lined face, it seemed she was hiding from the coldness of the soldiers around her as much as from the cold wind. They seemed to take forever to document her loved ones. When they stamped Samuel's passport and told him to move on, she walked eagerly toward the small family, tears in her eyes and her lips trembling with emotion. It had been a long nine years since she had seen them, and with the passing of her husband, she pined even more to embrace them once again.

Back at her meager apartment, Hilda poured her heart out to her cherished son and daughter-in-law. Since the Nazis had posted signs directing Germans to boycott Jewish businesses, even her most loyal customers had been afraid to support her. Their fears were justified. There were threats of murder, beatings occurred openly in the streets, and bricks had been thrown through her shop window twice. She had been afraid to mention what was happening in her letters to Samuel for fear of Nazi censors, who often took mail from the post office and opened it to identify any who weren't supportive of the Party.

As the family sat around the wooden table, she reached across and like a typical Jewish mother, took Samuel by both of his hands and said how pleased she was to see them. Even though Samuel was just as concerned, he tried to assure her that things would eventually turn out all right. The sound of a male voice in the home made her feel so much better.

Samuel and his family settled into life in Nazi Germany as best they could. To try to revive the family clothing store, Hilda officially retired from the business and transferred its ownership to her son. Samuel invested some of his savings into the small and ailing shop, changing its name, then advertising that it was now "American owned." Much to her relief, the change in ownership brought back a flood of old customers and set the business back on its feet.

Hilda would often sit in a wooden rocking chair knitting scarves and sweaters in a back room with the door slightly cracked, so that she could hear what was going on in the store. She loved watching Esther grow more confident in interacting with the customers. When the store became quiet, they would chat about the different characters who came in and their interesting traits. Some would have a little gossip to spread, while others were very quiet. One elderly man would saturate the store with a not-so-unpleasant smell of tobacco, after going through his daily ritual of filling his pipe and lighting it. He never failed to accidentally drop tobacco on the floor as he grasped it in his trembling fingers and stuffed it in the pipe.

Despite the presence of the Nazis, Samuel enjoyed the challenge of running a business, although he did have a problem with the language. He was in his early forties and found it difficult to learn a foreign dialect.

Jerry, however, picked up the language easier from talking with new friends who were fascinated that an American had come to their school. Jerry was a gangling kid; he looked like a younger version of his dad, but less weather-beaten and with a lot more hair. It was at school that he made one particularly close friend. His name was Karl von Ludendorff. Karl was different from the other boys his age. His friendship was more than a superficial fascination with the fact that Jerry came from the country where Hollywood movies were made and people drove big cars.

One day he asked Jerry if he would like to attend a church meeting with him. Although Jerry had been to the Ludendorff home a number of times over the years, he had never visited their church services. Jerry had attended church for a time back in Texas when he was younger, and when he asked his mother if he could go, she suggested that they go as a family.

As the four entered the von Ludendorff home early on Sunday morning, they were warmly welcomed and then ushered into the living room where about two dozen chairs were facing a wooden table. Though this was unlike any church service he'd ever experienced, when Jerry walked in, he felt strangely peaceful. On the table rested a large opened Bible, a small loaf of bread, and a silver cup.

"Fresh from the bakery this morning." Jerry turned to see a smiling Karl standing by the bread.

"Have you ever taken communion before?" Karl asked, as he walked toward him. Jerry explained that he had often taken communion when he attended a small Baptist church in Texas.

As the boys sat down, Karl told him that they were closely linked to the Baptists and that their church was called the International Bible Researchers. "Sounds impressive, doesn't it?" he laughed.

As they were talking Mr. von Ludendorff entered the room, winked at his son, leaned forward with an extended hand and said, "Jerry, good to see you! Welcome," in English, but laced with a strong German accent.

Jerry shook his hand and said in his best German, "Nice to see you again, sir." Karl's dad smiled warmly then looked at his wife chatting with Esther and Lillian, while Samuel flicked through a small book he had found on his chair. Mr. von Ludendorff greeted the family, shaking

Samuel's hand firmly as if he were an old friend. It was time to begin the meeting.

As the tall man stood behind the wooden table, the dozen or so regulars took their seats. He grinned broadly and said in his native tongue, "We are so excited to have such distinguished visitors with us this morning..." His voice then cracked with emotion. It was evident that he was feeling the strain of the Nazi oppression. He composed himself and continued, "We are truly thrilled to have members of the Adamson family with us today. After I open in prayer, for the sake of our honored guests the rest of the service will first be in German and then in English." Looking directly at the guests he added, "This is not only to help them understand what is going on, but to show off the English skills I picked up while studying in Great Britain some time ago." He smiled again, then opened in prayer.

Jerry hadn't mentioned to Karl that he hated attending church in Texas and that he went only because his mother made him go. As a child, he never understood why he had to sit for so long and listen to a boring minister. He used to stare at the second hand of his watch as it marched around the dial, then he would count the grooves in the paneling, bulbs in the ceiling lights, and ladies wearing hats. Jerry joked that church gave him a taste of "eternity," but today's service was different. Even if there had been grooves on the walls Jerry would have ignored them. The conviction in the voice of Mr. von Ludendorff held him spellbound.

As the man prayed, through squinted eyes, Jerry saw a tear slowly roll down his cheek. He spoke reverently and even though the prayer was in German Jerry could understand what he said: "We are so thankful for Your great mercy. Thank You for the mystery of Christ. Thank You for divine provision . . . for Your love. Help me today to speak Your mind, that Your people might be edified. Now Father, we lift up this nation. We pray for our people . . ."

His voice again cracked with emotion. He paused for a moment then continued, ". . . we pray for our people. May Your hand be upon them. We pray for the Nazis. Please touch this nation. Help us in this time of trial. May Your wonderful name be glorified in our lives, whether by life or by death. Amen."

The small congregation echoed "Amen," then there was a rustle of paper as Bibles were opened in anticipation of the sermon.

Mr. von Ludendorff began, "Today is a very special day for me. It is May 14, 1938, twenty years since I met my beloved bride. Twenty *wonderful* years." The small crowd watched with delight as he stepped forward, kissed his wife on the cheek, and said with a twinkle in his eye, "And today I love her with even more passion than when we first met." He then stepped back behind the homemade pulpit and continued, "We are going to look first at Romans 16:25, at the 'mystery, which was kept secret since the world began.'"

Jerry loved mysteries and listened with anticipation to what Mr. von Ludendorff would say next.

"This is a secret that God Himself has hidden from humanity from the beginning of the world," the preacher continued. "Not only does Paul speak of this mystery in the book of Romans, but also he writes in Ephesians chapter 3 verse 9, of 'the mystery which from the beginning of the world hath been hid in God.'" His face seemed to glow as he asked, "Do you know this extraordinary secret that God has hidden from the beginning of the world? Have you discovered the mystery?"

Jerry's curiosity was stirred. His old pastor was a walking cure for insomnia, but this man was rousing something deep in his heart. It was as though he had something to tell Jerry, something he was *supposed* to know.

"The apostle Paul also spoke of this hidden mystery in the book of Colossians. In his letter to them he mentioned, in chapter 1 verse 26, 'the mystery which hath been hid from ages and from generations.'" Mr. von Ludendorff looked up again, lifted his eyes above the congregation as though he were seeing something above their heads and said, "The Scriptures say, 'Awake thou that sleepest, and arise from the dead, and Christ shall give thee light.' Thank God that He gave 'light' to me as a young man of seventeen and revealed this incredible enigma. What is this most remarkable mystery? What is this amazing secret that God has hidden from all the eyes and ears of humanity?"

Jerry was intrigued. He felt like calling out, "Tell me what it is! Please tell me!"

Seeming to read Jerry's thoughts, the tall preacher smiled and said, "I am going to tell you what this mystery is. God hasn't left us in the dark. Please turn with me to——."

He paused mid-sentence and stared at his wife with a look of fear. Everyone knew what had stopped him from finishing his sentence. It was the sound of tires squealing to a halt, followed by the unmistakable sound of boots— *soldiers'* boots. Mr. von Ludendorff closed his eyes and whispered, "Dear God, please...not my children."

Suddenly the door burst open and Nazi soldiers filled the tiny room. They seized a family of four and thrust them outside. The officer in charge had papers in his hand and seemed to know exactly who he was looking for. It was strange that they were the only ones arrested.

Jerry felt sick with fear as a member of the Gestapo looked over his family's documents. After glaring at the small family, the officer stamped "May 14, 1938—SS" on their papers and spat out that they were to leave and never enter the home again.

The experience so scared Jerry, it was a date he vowed he would never forget. They didn't have to be told twice to leave.

The family had heard that in other parts of Germany the Nazis had entered church meetings and sent the people home, but they thought they were safe in Waldenberg.

At school, Jerry had another friend named Steffen, who wasn't as close to him as Karl. He'd had a different influence on Jerry's life. He was the one with whom he smoked cigarettes in the cramped hideout under the floor of the bakery.

Two days after the incident at church, Steffen banged on the Adamsons' door. When it was opened, wide-eyed and between breaths he sputtered, "They've taken away the von Ludendorffs!"

"Who has?" Mr. Adamson demanded.

The boy looked scared and said, "The Nazis!"

Samuel knew that, as pacifists, the von Ludendorffs had refused to teach their children Nazi ideology. He heard that after the church service had been broken up, there was some sort of court hearing set in motion. He discovered the details in that night's newspaper. Under the headline "Enemies of the State" he read:

Waldenberg: The courts have had children removed from their parents. They deemed two members of a Christian sect called "The International Bible Researchers," Mr. and Mrs. Otto von Ludendorff, unfit to be parents of their two children. The court accused them of creating an environment where the children would grow up as *enemies of the state*. The children were surrendered into the state's care. The judge delivered a lengthy statement reading in part, "The law as a racial and national instrument entrusts German parents with the education of their children only under certain conditions, namely, that they educate them in the fashion that the nation and the state expect."

Samuel looked up at Esther. She could see the concern in his eyes. He put the newspaper down and gazed toward the door, then back at her. "We've got to leave this place," he said.

CHAPTER TWO
THE REIGN OF THE REICH

❧

WITHIN A WEEK, Samuel sold the clothing business to a German banker and purchased a car. Then he, his family, and his mother headed for Poland, relieved to be leaving Germany. Some years earlier, Hitler had amassed the largest ever gathering at a Nazi rally in Nuremberg. The streets were lined with storm troopers, and church bells chimed as Hitler arrived for the opening of the National Socialist Congress. The Führer reviewed an incredible parade of 600,000 men. Back then Samuel couldn't help but think, "Why on earth would that madman gather so many troops if he wasn't planning to take Europe, and perhaps the world?"

Samuel and his family would stay in the Polish city of Krakow, in the home of his Jewish cousin, until the U.S. Immigration and Naturalization Service sorted out a few "complexities" in his mother's application to immigrate. Little did he know that it would be a two-year battle with the U.S. bureaucracy. It seemed that America didn't want Germans migrating to the United States. They could see how volatile things were in Europe, and after a rally of 20,000 German-American Nazis took place at Madison Square Garden in New York, they virtually closed the doors. America had too many Nazi sympathizers.

Samuel's cousin, Joseph Greenberg, was a cheerful man. He had changed his name to Joe Ackerman after his relatives were arrested, and now looked a little out of place in Krakow dressed like a stereotypical Texan. He was a tall man with a prominent belly, standing six foot two inches, and a large moustache that reminded Samuel of the horns on longhorn cattle. He didn't wear a ten-gallon hat, but he insisted on wearing his well-worn boots that he had brought with him many years earlier when he emigrated.

Joseph had never cared what people thought of him when he was a child. Samuel remembered him when he lived in Texas. He was always trying to entertain people, either by wearing bizarre hats with feathers sticking out of them, or by telling jokes and laughing. He had an endless stream of jokes. He would burst into a room and say, "I have six eyes, three ears, and two noses. What am I?" When people couldn't guess, he would say, "*Really* ugly!" and run from the room. He still delighted in making people laugh, although his concerns about the Nazis weighed heavily on him.

Samuel too was deeply concerned in Poland as he carefully followed what was happening back in Germany. Early in 1938, Hitler promoted himself to military chief giving him unprecedented power. He named himself the "Supreme Commander of the armed forces," and seized direct control of foreign policy. In March 1938, he returned to Austria, his native homeland, and proclaimed *Anschluss*—a union between Austria and Germany. Any opponents were immediately arrested. Hitler held a referendum and concluded that 99 percent of the Austrian people approved of the confederation.

Joseph told Samuel that on April 26, Hitler had passed a law requiring all Jews to declare their assets. Those who failed to comply could receive a hard-labor prison sentence of ten years, as well as having all their possessions seized by the Nazis. Joseph said that his German relatives were terrified and immediately complied. They had to identify the amounts and locations of their savings, describe jewelry they owned with its estimated value, and even give details of insurance policies. They were forced to list *everything* of value. He then said that, despite their compliance, every one of his relatives had been arrested and sent to concentration camps.

Samuel slowly put both of his hands onto his forehead, closed his eyes, and sighed deeply. "That's why! That's why the Gestapo took away that family of four from church that day," he told Joseph. "They knew who they were looking for because of that detailed disclosure. They knew exactly how much they were worth because, like millions of other Jews, they had revealed it in detail a few weeks earlier. I think those who filled out those forms were filling out their own death warrants!"

In October of the same year, Hitler's troops marched into Sudetenland, a border area of Czechoslovakia. Large crowds lined the boulevards, waving Nazi banners and tossing flowers into the street as they greeted the Führer. Germany had been given that area, occupied mainly by ethnic Germans, in the Munich Agreement signed in September, but Hitler was not content with that expansion.

In March 1939, the Nazi cancer spread even further—into Prague, the capital of Czechoslovakia. Hitler then divided up the country into several regions, each under the reign of the Third Reich. His entry into the city was not as celebrated as in Austria or Sudetenland. Many jeered at the soldiers and others wept openly as the swastika was raised above the buildings. A curfew was immediately put into effect. Public buildings and banks were taken over by Germans and the Gestapo fanned through the city with lists in their hands.

Samuel was alarmed at what he could see slowly happening. Hitler was taking Europe with little resistance, and because no blood was seen to be spilled, the world leaders were tolerating his fanaticism.

Samuel, however, wasn't the only one who could see the time bomb ticking. He was heartened to read that half a million people lined the streets in New York to watch a "Stop Hitler" march with 20,000 participants. Through BBC radio he heard that the British Prime Minister, Neville Chamberlain, informed Poland, "Should the Polish government feel that its independence be threatened to such an extent that it had to resist by force, Poland would find Britain and France on her side."

It was only because of the knowledge that Hitler would be kept in line by the threats of Britain and France that Samuel and his family remained in Poland. Had he known how insane the man was and what was about to happen, he would have immediately left the country.

Chamberlain's proclamation merely stirred the demons in Hitler. He told 100,000 of his followers at a rally that Germany would not allow Britain to initiate its "devilish plan." In May of that year, the Führer signed an alliance with Italy, a union that was referred to as a "Pact of Steel." Then he shocked leaders of Western Europe by signing a non-aggression treaty with the Russians. He boasted that the treaty thwarted Britain's efforts to form a circle around Germany.

That left Poland isolated in Eastern Europe. Britain evacuated thousands of children out of London, and France whisked their children out of Paris and awaited the inevitable.

CHAPTER THREE
ECHOES OF THUNDER

❦

A FTER TWENTY-ONE years of peace, Europe was suddenly thrust into war again. A massive German force of 1.25 million men swept across the Polish border on September 1, 1939. Russian troops invaded from the east and Poland began to fall into the hands of a merciless enemy. Britain and France quickly declared war on Germany, fulfilling their defensive obligations to Poland. In a communiqué, the two nations said they invaded to bring order to Poland and to help the Polish people confronted with the collapse of their state.

Three weeks of nightmarish bombing left Warsaw in devastation. The Nazis called the invasion its *Blitzkrieg*—a "Lightning War." The name was certainly appropriate. By the end of September, 60,000 Poles had been killed by the

Nazi invasion, 200,000 more were wounded, and 700,000 soldiers were being held in captivity.

Krakow was one of the first cities to be assaulted. Samuel mistakenly thought that the Polish troops would hold back the enemy front, and that Britain would come to their aid. But the truth was that he and his beloved family were now trapped. If they went south they would confront hostile Hungarian troops sympathetic to the Nazi cause. Since the invasion, he had no idea where the U.S. stood militarily. If they had entered the conflict, then his U.S. documentation would be a death warrant. If his family went east, they would face Russian troops who were as merciless as the Nazis. The Germans had taken Bromberg to the north.

The only safe option was to stay where they were and pray—and pray they did. That night Samuel wept openly, and took his family in his arms and pleaded with God for their safekeeping. Jerry had never seen his dad like this before. Until now he had scoffed at any thought of faith in God.

Samuel's knowledge of Germany's recent history added to his dread. The Nazis were so coldly systematic...like a disease insidiously spreading throughout a human body. They had persecuted the Jews in stages. He remembered reading in U.S. newspapers how it began well before World War II, with legislation that systematically removed Jews from society. Following Hitler's takeover of power on January 30, 1933, he began his first nationwide Jewish boycott. Nazis stood outside Jewish businesses throughout Germany to intimidate Jews. The boycott wasn't particularly successful, yet it was declared to have served its purpose and ended after one day. Samuel remembered seeing a translation of one of the boycott posters:

German people's comrades!
German housewives!
You all know the disgraceful methods that so-called "German" Jews abroad are using to incite against the German people and Adolf Hitler's national government. If we do not want to give up and sink into deeper misery, we *must* defend ourselves. We therefore call on you to heed the appeal of our Führer, the German people's chancellor, for a *boycott against the Jews* and expect the full support of each person in this defensive action.

Do not buy from Jewish shops!

Do not go to a Jewish doctor!

But maintain the strictest disci-
pline. Do not even touch the hair on a
Jew's head. The boycott begins Satur-
day morning at 10:00 a.m. From that
moment on, we will watch to ensure
that the boycott is strictly followed. He
who tries to ignore the boycott will be
seen as an *enemy* of the German people.

The American media reported that the boycott had failed and that the Nazis would back
off. But they didn't. Instead, the Nazis began a
concerted effort to change Germany's percep-
tion of Jews. They portrayed Hitler as a savior,
equating his "deliverance" of the German people to the biblical exodus from Egypt, while the
place of the Jewish people in other Old Testament accounts was distorted. A Nazi educational
slide set included an image called "David and
Goliath." It showed a stereotypically drawn "Jewish" David crouching naked and Neanderthal-
like behind a bush, while his opponent, the
giant Goliath, loomed in Aryan splendor before
him. And in one of the most famous speeches
of his career, to the German Reichstag on January 30, 1939, Hitler assumed the role of a Hebrew
prophet, calling down destruction on a sinful

Jewish people. His words echoed a theme common in anti-Jewish "Christian" literature of the time. The Old Testament, some of its defenders argued, was to be salvaged, not because it honored or glorified the Jews, but precisely because its prophets and punishments proved God's displeasure with those "stiffnecked" people. In a 1939 flyer they were painted as being "destructive Jews" and likened to those in the time of Christ—"the same Jewish criminal people who nailed Christ to the cross!"

In Krakow, Samuel's family heard the constant and terrifying sounds of war. Echoes of thunder came closer and closer to Joseph's home where they were staying. On the third day after the invasion, very early in the morning, Hilda awoke to the sound of gunfire. She climbed out of bed to peer out her small window.

In the predawn she could see soldiers arresting people in the adjacent street and lining them up for questioning. Her eyes squinted as she tried to see if she could recognize any of them. As she did so, she whispered to herself, "It's just the men..." She jumped as she felt a hand on her shoulder and glanced around to see Samuel. "They're going to question the men," she told him, trying not to sound alarmed.

He shook his head and soberly whispered, "*No…*" His mother looked questioningly into his deep brown eyes. Just then she flinched at the sound of guns being fired in unison and looked back to see about a dozen men fall to the ground. She put her hand to her mouth and gasped, "Dear God, they've shot them!"

The voices of his father and grandmother through the paper-thin walls had been enough to wake Jerry, who had gotten up and slipped on some clothes. When he heard the shots, he burst out of his room. Samuel ran across the hall, grabbed him by the arm and said, "They're shooting the men! We've got to hide bef—."

A loud pounding on the front door made their hearts stop in terror. By now Hilda had come into the hallway. She whispered, "The back door, *quickly!*"

Samuel opened the door, pushed his son ahead of him and said, "Run, Jerry! Run for your dear life!"

∽∾

TWELVE LONG, cold, pain-filled hours passed beneath the floor of the bakery. The bleeding from Jerry's shoulder wound had stopped, but not until after he had lost enough blood to make him dizzy and weak. By now it was dusk and the horrifying sounds of war had quieted down. The firing squads, which throughout the day could be heard about every ten minutes, had mercifully stopped.

It took some time to maneuver his injured body back through the small opening into which he had crawled. As he stood to his feet for the first time in a dozen hours, his head spun and he stumbled into the wooden crates beside him, knocking them noisily to the ground and sending a wave of fear through his mind. Had anyone heard him?

Three minutes later, he stood in the shadows beside the back window of Joseph's house. The curtains were drawn but he could hear male German voices coming from the living room. There was a tiny gap in the curtain, but he was fearful to lean across the window to look in, in case he was seen. Were his mother and his sister okay? Did his father escape? What had happened to his grandmother and Joseph? Whose voices could he hear?

His concern for his family partially overcame his fears and he slowly leaned over and peered into the home. To Jerry's relief, two Nazis stood with their backs to the window so they didn't notice him. From what he could see through the small window, they were officers of the Third Reich. His mother and sister were huddled together in a corner. *Thank God they were alive.* The officers, who were stationed there while awaiting orders from the front, laughed as they drank their foaming mugs of beer, then one reached into his pocket and pulled out a coin and tossed it into the air. Jerry's heart sank with pity as he saw the fear in the eyes of both women. One of the officers then walked across to Lillian and lifted her from the floor. A thought flashed across the boy's mind: *Rape!* He mouthed, "Dear God, no! Please don't let this happen."

Jerry experienced a wave of emotion he had never felt before. He was outraged that these animals would assault his beloved mother and sister. His fury seemed to overcome his fears and clear his mind.

It was then that he remembered a gun his father had brought with him from the U.S. The loaded handgun was hidden under a loose floorboard in the bathroom. Quickly he made his way to the bathroom window and pried it open.

For the first time since he was shot he wasn't aware of pain in his arm as a reserve of adrenaline pumped through his body. He quietly slid down onto the floor, dropped to his knees in the darkened room, and slowly pried up the loose floorboard. He felt for the gun and for a moment feared it was gone, but then his fingers touched its smooth surface. He grasped the cold steel and held it firmly in his hand. Only once before had his father let him touch it, and that was to show him how to release the safety mechanism, if the time ever came that he needed to.

In the semi-darkness, he carefully flipped the safety with his left hand and held the gun tightly in his right. He then quietly opened the bathroom door, entered the dark hallway and deliberately stopped for a moment to calm his thoughts.

As he stood in the hallway, he could hear the pathetic cries of his sister coming from one of the bedrooms. Gritting his teeth in rage, he turned the familiar handle and pushed open the door to see the dark figure of a man pressing his terrified sister against the wall. He had his back to Jerry, had hold of both of Lillian's wrists and was forcing himself upon her. The officer looked for a moment at the change of expression on Lillian's face as she saw Jerry. He then turned his head and mumbled something in German, thinking it was the other officer. But when he saw Jerry's figure standing with a raised gun, terror filled his eyes. He released Lillian and scrambled for his revolver.

Jerry fired two shots into his chest, then ran to his sister and pulled her up from the floor. As he did so, he heard a voice say in German, "Uncooperative, huh?" as the other officer, hearing the shots, appeared in the doorway. Jerry took careful aim at the silhouette and fired. One bullet pierced the man's upper chest, and as he crumpled to the ground, Jerry put another bullet into his back.

Then Jerry collapsed in exhaustion.

It was morning before he regained consciousness. The distant sounds of war had become louder as it neared the small home. However, there were no more firing squads in the area—probably because there were no more men in the vicinity who were left alive. As Jerry opened his eyes, the first words from his lips were, "Dad . . . is Dad okay?"

His mother seemed to look right through him as she replied, "Your father's dead."

As the first shots came as they ran from the home the previous morning, one bullet penetrated Samuel's leg and put him on the ground;

another hit Jerry. The next two shots Jerry heard a moment later went through the back of his father's head, as the Nazi soldiers mercilessly ignored his pleas that he was an American citizen. Esther, Lillian, and Hilda stood in the doorway in unspeakable horror and witnessed the incident. To the soldiers, Samuel was just another raving Jew, and Jews were to be exterminated. Some went quietly; others protested.

After seeing Jerry, bloody, run around the corner, the women resigned themselves to the fact that he was also dead. They were more than astonished to see him show up at night with a gun in his hand, and kill the two Nazis.

They then filled him in on the events that had taken place that day. Joseph had been dragged from his bedroom and shot along with six other men right in front of the house. Their bodies were later picked up by a truck and hauled away. Around mid-morning, two members of the Gestapo pounded on the door and demanded to see the women's documents. When they discovered Samuel's mother was a Jew, other officers arrested her on the spot and said that she was to be sent to a concentration camp.

When Jerry had gained his composure, he asked where the bodies of the officers were. In the blackness of the night, the two women had loaded them into their car and dumped them about a mile from the home.

Jerry pressed his hands against his face in grief over the deaths of his beloved father and Joseph and the arrest of his grandmother. He then heaved a deep sigh of relief regarding the officers, and reached around to clutch his aching shoulder. Looking down at a clean bandage, he noted, "You two have done a good job."

CHAPTER FOUR
BLOOD, TOIL, AND TEARS

∽◦∾

I T HAD BEEN three weeks since Samuel was killed, and in that short time Jerry matured from a sixteen-year-old boy into a man. He had to. After losing precious members of their family, he felt he needed to be strong to lead his grieving mother and sister, and he had to be brave.

During those three weeks, despite the risks involved, they took turns driving south into Hungary, west through occupied Austria, and then into France. They could either stay and be sitting ducks, or take their chances in flight. They chose the latter. Fortunately for them America was still neutral, and their documents got them through six tightly secured border patrols. While their hearts skipped with relief at being allowed through, many times they saw the heartbreaking sight of Jewish men, women, and children being rounded up like cattle, both in Hungary and in Austria.

Once in France, Esther used their savings to rent a small apartment and buy food. They still had most of the proceeds from the sale of the store, in addition to Hilda's assets; she didn't trust banks and had kept quite a bundle in a secret hiding place. The family kept a close eye on what news they could find. They heard that six people had been killed in Munich on November 8, 1939, when a bomb exploded in a packed hall of Nazi veterans. The bomb had been intended for Hitler, but he had left the hall 15 minutes earlier than expected. In Prague, on November 24, the Gestapo executed 120 students they accused of anti-Nazi plotting.

By now, Jerry was growing frustrated and disappointed that the U.S. still hadn't joined the war. Back in the States a group of "isolationists" had formed what they called the America First Committee, counting among its members such high-profile figures as the famed Charles Lindbergh, Robert McCormick (publisher of the *Chicago Tribune*), and a few U.S. senators. Their powerful voices opposed American intervention in what was referred to as "the European war," yet Jerry knew that only if the Western nations banded together could they defeat fascism.

A few months after Samuel's death, Esther longed to get back to the security of their home in the United States. Their family no longer had any ties to Europe, and she wanted them to leave as soon as they could. With the U.S. economy picking up a bit, she was hopeful that they could once again make a living there.

The kids, however, were enthralled with Paris, and wanted to stay a few more weeks to enjoy a bit of the summer in France. Having spent most of their "growing up" years in Europe, they were not as anxious to return to the Texas farm they had left behind six years earlier. At 18 Lillian was now an adult, and Jerry a responsible 16, and the two managed to convince their mother that they were mature enough to stay safely in France while she went on ahead.

Esther reluctantly left them the first week of May. It turns out she got out of Europe by the skin of her teeth. Numerous attacks began shortly after she left, making it unsafe to travel.

On May 10, 1940, Hitler began attacking Holland and Belgium with his *Blitzkrieg*. Jerry huddled close to an old wireless radio and listened to the BBC report that hundreds of Nazi planes had swooped over their cities, dropping German parachutists often dressed in Dutch military uniforms. Holland's queen was outraged at his betrayal and issued a statement: "After our country, with scrupulous conscientiousness, had observed strict neutrality…, Germany made a sudden attack on our territory without warning."

The Belgium Prime Minister declared a "state of alarm," hoping that Britain and France would come to their aid. The reason for the attacks, Hitler claimed, was that he believed Britain and France were about to use these countries as steppingstones to invade Germany. "The Allies were preparing an onslaught on Germany which the Reich could not tolerate," the German Foreign Minister declared. "In the life-and-death struggle thrust upon the German people, the Government does not intend to await an attack by Britain and France."

It took only two weeks for Germany to conquer Holland and Belgium, bringing the Nazi war machine to the edge of the English Channel. The Allies, fully aware of what was next on Hitler's agenda, had every reason to be nervous. France's Premier Paul Reynaud was grieved at the fall of the two countries, saying that their surrender made the situation "dark" and "grave."

The following day Jerry heard that President Roosevelt, in an effort to prepare for the worst—America's direct involvement in the war—had announced plans to train 50,000 military pilots. Congress supported him, and passed legislation backing his proposal. It was this awareness, and the first speech by Britain's new Prime Minister, that made Jerry want to stay in France and do all he could to stop the onslaught of Nazism. As he tuned into the BBC, he heard the distinctive sound of Winston Churchill. "I have nothing to offer, but blood, toil, tears, and sweat," Churchill intoned. His voice moved something deep in Jerry's heart.

The month of June was an unspeakably depressing one for France and for the two young Americans. On the third of the month, two hundred German planes dropped a total of eleven hundred bombs on Paris, killing many. Fortunately, none came close to Jerry and Lillian although they could hear the continual, terrifying explosions. Then, to their horror, the two heard reports that German soldiers, fighting their way across Northern France, had trapped 340,000 Allied troops on the beaches of Dunkirk. The ruthless and confident Germans forced back the battle-weary British, French, and Belgian divisions to a point where it looked like they would be annihilated.

When the French and British troops had rushed to the defense of Belgium and Holland and the countries surrendered, it exposed their left flank. Hitler's forces took advantage of the opportunity and stormed through the gaping hole, trapping the Allies. Although around 130,000 died, the Royal Air Force fought an air battle against the *Luftwaffe* (German air force), which gave time for an evacuation that was hailed as the "miracle of Dunkirk." In nine days, a massive Allied effort pulled 340,000 grateful troops back across the channel. It was a bittersweet victory.

The evening of June 4, as Jerry tuned in to the BBC, he was stirred once again by the words of Winston Churchill. "We shall fight on the seas and oceans," Churchill vowed, despite the evacuation. "We shall fight, with growing confidence and strength, in the air. We shall defend our island, whatever the cost may be. We shall fight on the beaches, we shall fight on the landing grounds, we shall fight in the fields and in the streets, we shall fight in the hills; we shall never surrender."

All-too-familiar tears rolled down Jerry's cheeks, partly because of such soul-stirring words, but also because he felt fearful not just for himself and his sister, but for France. They'd been in France for less than a year, but he had fallen in love with the few people he had befriended, and even more so he had fallen in love with Paris. There was something special about the city, with its wide winding river, its magnificent architecture, cobblestone streets, outdoor cafés, and wonderful tree-lined streets, not to mention the Eiffel Tower, planted like a king in the center of a colorful city chessboard.

His fears were justified. What was considered unthinkable a few years earlier had now happened. Darkness had fallen over the "City of Light." *Hitler invaded Paris.* The beautiful city was being attacked by an obsessive and murderous madman. It took a mere ten days for the Germans to take Paris after they began the Battle of France.

The tears continued to flow as Jerry stood under the trees and watched the German armored cars sweep down the Champs Elysees. His heart almost broke when his eyes fixed upon a sign plastered on the Eiffel Tower: *Deutschland siegt auf Allen Fronten.* He didn't need anyone to help with the translation: "Germany conquers on all fronts."

∽○∾

THE 1940 SURRENDER of France to Hitler was devastating to many in the country, who felt betrayed by their government. It had not only failed militarily in securing the country's borders, but had allowed the creation of the Nazi-approved Vichy government in the central and southern regions. This sense of betrayal was the catalyst that began the French Resistance movement, which would help to fight the Germans and provide the Allies with vital intelligence and assistance. Rather than attempting to return to America, Jerry and Lillian, who were both passionate about the Nazi occupation, wanted to remain in Paris and join this new movement.

But the French, it turned out, were not as welcoming as Jerry and Lillian had hoped. Many were bitter that the United States had stayed out of the conflict. Despite attempts the two made to contact the Resistance, they were unsuccessful. As far as the French were concerned, any American who had lived for any length of time in Germany shouldn't be trusted. Jerry couldn't blame them for their mistrust. Paris crawled with both Germans and Frenchmen who would betray the Resistance for a price.

It was only after getting a job serving tables in a small outdoor cafe that Lillian finally made contact with the underground, through a man named Marc. As she cleared a table one afternoon, without looking up from a newspaper he was reading, he directed her attention to a man in his early thirties who was sitting at a nearby table drinking coffee. Marc had heard through reliable sources that this man had connections with the Resistance.

Lillian scribbled "Long live France...I *must* speak with you" in French on a piece of paper. She put it on a saucer and took it to the man's table. Ten minutes later, she returned to clear the table, lifted the cup and saw what she had prayed for. There was another small piece of paper. In the kitchen, she carefully unfolded it and read the words: "124 Bordeaux 7 p.m. Alone."

Lillian's heart raced as she knocked on the door of 124 Bordeaux that evening. A smiling woman answered and asked in French, "Did you come alone?" Lillian assured her that she did.

Inside, two men and a woman were playing cards and took no notice as Lillian stepped inside and shut the door.

"My name is Marian," the woman at the door said. "What would you like me to do for you?"

"I want to join the Resistance. Can you help me?"

Marian gave a small laugh and asked, "Now why would an American girl, who can't yet be out of her teenage years, want to join the French Resistance?"

"Because the Nazis killed my father and sent my grandmother to a concentration camp."

One of the men tossed a card onto the center of the table and without looking up asked, "How do we know you are speaking the truth?"

"You don't," Lillian said.

Smiling, he turned to look at her and said, "Why then should we trust you?"

Marian whispered loud enough for all to hear, "I trust her."

After a few moments the man told Lillian, "We will contact you at your work." Then he nodded to the woman to see her to the door. The meeting lasted only two minutes, yet it sent Lillian's heart racing again, this time with excitement.

That night Lillian thanked God for the meeting, and then opened a Bible she had brought with her from Poland. It was the Bible her father had started reading while they waited and prayed that the British and the French would reach them before the Germans. She began reading, something she would do every night from then on.

The next day, and the next, she lifted a hundred coffee cups looking for a note. Each time her disappointment grew.

A week passed and still no one contacted her. It was evident that they didn't trust her. Just when she had resigned herself to the fact that there would be no communication, she saw a small folded note as she lifted a cup. On it she read: "If you would like to join our card game, come to 73 La Havre at 7:30 tonight. We need only one player so come alone."

Lillian put the note into her pocket, then whispered, "Thank you, Lord."

CHAPTER FIVE
FAMILY CAMPS

∽∘∾

J EAN MOULIN, the French underground leader, looked directly at Jerry and asked, "Why aren't the Americans helping us?"

Jerry also felt impatient with the reticence of the U.S. to fight alongside the Allies. He could identify with the Frenchman's frustration. "With the fall of France we had hoped that Roosevelt would drop his policy of isolationism," he said. "Many back home are feeling very nervous about what's happening in Europe. I don't know what will have to happen to bring the United States into the war, but whatever it takes, I hope it will come quickly."

Jean's question came in light of the fact that Italy's Premier Mussolini united his country with Germany against Britain and France. On June 10, 1940, President Roosevelt responded by saying, "The hand that held the dagger has struck it into the back of its neighbor."

Jean gave a brave smile, put a fatherly arm around Lillian and said, "Still, it's good to have you two with us." Once the Resistance realized that Lillian could be trusted, they welcomed her and her brother.

Jean was a kind and courageous man. Earlier that month the Germans had arrested him for refusing to sign a statement blaming Senegalese soldiers for murders committed by the Germans. While he was in prison, a German soldier had scribbled a note to him saying, "I compliment you on the energy with which you defend your country's honor." He had also been instrumental in uniting the Resistance fighters in the North and the South.

Lillian looked up at him and said, "I had given up hope of you ever contacting me. I didn't think you trusted me."

"We didn't," Jean said with a smile. "We tailed you for a week. We also checked up on where you came from. The fact is, we seldom allow anyone to join the underground if they don't come with a concrete *personal* recommendation."

He smiled warmly at Jerry. "Your sister's word was good enough for us to trust you. We are very pleased to have a small part of America with us."

That night about a dozen members of the Resistance sat and listened to the BBC as General Charles de Gaulle was speaking from London. "Whatever happens," he said resolutely, "the flame of the French Resistance must not go out, and it will not go out."

IN SEPTEMBER, Germany began a "Blitz" of sustained air attacks against Britain, bombing them repeatedly for over eight months. At one time an incredible 60,000 buildings were destroyed. As the attacks continued, an estimated one million homes were damaged or destroyed in London alone.

In Warsaw, Poland, all Jews had been ordered to wear a six-point Star of David outlined with the word "Jew," which was to be visibly worn on their clothing. In October, the Germans herded the Jewish population behind a ten-foot wall enclosing the city's ghetto district. The Nazis said they were giving the Jews a "new life" in what they called "family camps."

Hitler, meanwhile, invaded and conquered Yugoslavia the following April after a massive bombing attack. Then in June, in what was seen as an insane move, he attacked his own ally—Russia—and encircled Leningrad, planning to starve the city to death.

The United States finally joined the war after the Japanese devastated Pearl Harbor in Hawaii with a 360-plane surprise attack. The aerial strike was extremely successful, but Japanese submarines failed to finish off the wounded ships inside the harbor. Although Japan had deceived the U.S. by expressing interest in continued peace, the success of the attack surprised the Japanese as much as the Americans. Over 2,400 Americans were killed, with an additional 1,300 wounded. President Franklin D. Roosevelt declared that day, December 7, 1941, was "a date which will live in infamy," and the following day Congress declared war on Japan. For Jerry, Pearl Harbor was bittersweet.

Jerry was also hearing reports that Jews throughout Europe were being slaughtered en masse in the dreaded concentration camps, something Nazis called "the final solution." Hitler said that it was the only fate deserved by the *Untermenschen*—the subhumans. In many concentration camps, German physicians carried out cruel experiments on their prisoners.

One of these "doctors" was the notorious Josef Mengele, who worked in Auschwitz. His experiments included putting victims in pressure chambers, using them as guinea pigs for drug tests, freezing them, attempting to change their eye color by injecting chemicals into children's eyes, and various amputations and other brutal surgeries. Those who managed to survive his horrific experiments were almost always killed and dissected shortly afterward. Jerry feared that his beloved grandmother had been sent to this infamous death camp, and he was horrified at the thought of what had happened to her.

THERE WAS A sudden knock on the door at the Resistance hideout. It was Henri, one of the members, carrying a newspaper as he stepped inside. Lifting his arms in despair in typical French fashion, he slapped the newspaper onto the wooden table and said with disgust, "I don't believe it! I don't believe it! The man is insane!"

By now both Lillian and Jerry were well versed in French, even when it was spoken with such passion. Jean picked up the newspaper and muttered a profanity. The article he saw read: "At 3:00 this morning, thousands of French police officers fanned out through Paris on an unprecedented mission. They rounded up 13,000 Jews, loaded them into buses, and locked them up in the sports facility known as the Winter Velodrome. Among the people cowering beneath the bleachers are invalids, pregnant women, and more than 3,000 children. The round-up was part of an agreement Vichy's Pierre Laval made with the Nazis. The Germans agreed not to deport any French Jews to Germany if the French arrested foreign Jews. Laval claims he can save 75,000 lives. Critics say that he has bartered with the devil."

The critics, it turns out, were right. Reports were filtering back from Warsaw about the "new life" the Jews were given in Poland's ghettos. Over 400,000 were confined to a 1.3-square-mile area, and were forced to live in horrifying conditions where about one out of four died of starvation or disease. Most were killed or dragged to the Treblinka concentration camp where they were executed.

Jewish resistance fighters, who were able to keep one step ahead of the Nazis, returned to Warsaw with stories from the ghetto at Lublin. From their apartment windows, Jews there could see the fearful sight of the barbed wire of the Majdanak concentration camp, as well as the smoke rising from the large crematoriums. As the Jews began to realize what happened to those who were taken to the concentration camps, when the Nazis came for more in January 1943, over 60,000 ghetto residents resisted them. Yet the Jews in the walled ghetto had nowhere to hide.

SS troops attacked the Warsaw ghetto in April with orders to deport the remainder to a forced labor camp. When they entered the area, they began searching it systematically, block by block, house to house, basement to ceiling. When there was resistance, the SS opened fire with tanks, mortars, and machineguns, or they torched the homes with flame-throwers.

Word leaked back around the middle of May that there were no more Jews left in the Warsaw ghetto. General Jurgen Stroop reported that his troops captured or killed over 55,000 Jews, but not all of that number died from Nazi bullets. Many chose to remain in their burning homes; others jumped from their roofs.

Around that time, Andre, one of the trusted members of the Resistance, disappeared. After making extensive inquiries, Jean concluded that the Nazis had captured and killed him. Little did he know that something worse had happened.

As Andre was leaving his home one morning, he was stopped by two members of the SS, arrested and driven to the outskirts of Paris. There he was ushered into a small room of a large, stone church building. The room contained two high-ranking Nazi officers and the smell of stale cigar smoke.

He was ordered to sit in a chair in front of a large desk. Through an interpreter, he was informed that the Germans had proof he was a member of the French Underground, and that they would let him go if he would merely give the address of Jean Moulin. Andre forced a smile and said he would *never* betray the Resistance.

One of the officers then stood up, walked around to the front of the desk and sat casually on its edge. He was holding two large photographs. He glanced at them and said in broken French, "Oh, I think you will." He looked directly at the Frenchman and handed him the prints.

Andre's heart sank as he stared at pictures of his beloved wife and two young daughters. Jean had bent the rules and allowed Andre to join the Resistance only on the condition that he would send his wife and children out of the country. He was fearful that if any of its members had families, they would die by the hands of Nazis. Andre had made the mistake of sending his beloved family to what he thought was a secret location in southern Italy.

The officer walked back around his desk and sat down. "At this moment," he threatened, "we have your wife and two little girls in the hands of the SS in Barletta. If you simply write the address of Jean Moulin on this piece of paper, we will immediately take them back to their home. However, if you fail to cooperate with us, we will be forced to execute them. Your wife will be questioned and then hanged, and your two children drowned. Then we will torture you until you tell us what we want to know... *and you will tell us everything*, believe me.

"However, if you do decide to be sensible and help us, we will take you to Italy to be reunited with your family. You have until noon to make up your mind what you will do." He then stood up from the desk and left the room.

Andre's head spun with confusion. It was as though his whole life suddenly came crashing in on him. If he cooperated, he would be a traitor to his country, and *if he didn't*... He leaned forward and thumped the desk in anger.

For three hours Andre was anguished as he wrestled with his options. He wept aloud. He cursed. He prayed. He contemplated suicide by smashing the glass from the barred window high above the officer's desk and cutting his wrists. But what good would that do? They would see that as a refusal to cooperate and kill his family anyway.

When the SS officer entered the room, Andre was bent double with his head in his hands. The officer took Andre's right hand and put a pencil in it. He looked at the Nazi with utter disdain, then down at the blank piece of paper on the desk in front of him. He leaned forward and with a trembling hand wrote an address on the paper.

On July 8, 1943, the Germans announced that Jean Moulin, the leader of the French Resistance, was dead. He had been tortured for a month. He was age forty-four.

Lillian had been seen with Jean the evening he was arrested. There were rumors that she had also been arrested then sent to a concentration camp.

CHAPTER SIX
TALL ORDER

"WE WANT HIM killed but we don't want any holes in the uniform!"

It was a strange order, but an important one.

Churchill himself had requested that the Resistance find out exactly where the aircraft assembly plants were located in Berlin, and Jerry was well qualified for the task of finding out that information. The Allies wanted detailed maps for their bombers, and he was familiar with Berlin as he had visited the city often with his father while in Waldenberg. The war had stolen Jerry's teenage years and thrust him into premature manhood, but he looked the part. In a matter of a few years it seems his grandfather's genes had kicked in. He remembers hearing how his granddad was a tall, hairy individual, who, as a youth, looked much older than his age. With his good looks and a keen mind, Jerry could pass as an officer. He had also picked up the German language very quickly, as he had with French, and most important, he could be trusted to get the job done. All that was needed was a uniform to fit a man who was six feet tall and the ID to go with it.

In accordance with the tall order, two members of the Resistance followed a lanky SS officer as he walked out of a club late one night and down a lonely street toward one of the many brothels of Paris. It was unusual to see a Nazi officer in that part of town by himself, but he was obviously drunk and therefore not too concerned about what could happen to him. The man was so inebriated, one of the Frenchmen merely had to whisper, "Hey, Fritz," and when the soldier turned toward him, the other quickly put a piece of wire around his neck and pulled tight. It was quick, quiet, and clean...the uniform was delivered in perfect condition.

Jerry was straining at the bit to do something big to frustrate the Nazi cause. He was distraught at the death of Jean and the disappearance of Lillian, and couldn't get his sister out of his mind—not that he wanted to. Had she too been killed, or sent to a dreaded concentration camp? Or was she being held for questioning and tortured? He had gone from contact to contact, discreetly asking questions hoping for some light, but to no avail. It was a horrible feeling that weighed heavily on Jerry. In addition to Jean's death, there was the death of his beloved father, Hilda, and Joseph, and now he lost his only sibling, to whom he was very close. He felt as though part of him had died, and it fueled his determination to do whatever he could to stop Hitler's madness.

The plan was to drop him by parachute in a field about three miles east of Berlin. The Allies had flown many bombing raids over the area. They would go at night, fly high, and carefully drop Jerry into the right location. He would have to bury his parachute, make his own way to the city, and locate as many assembly plants as he could within one week. Then he would have to get back to the airfield to be picked up at 1900 hours, seven nights later. The only way they could possibly carry out such a dangerous assignment was for the plane to land and take off in thick fog, something that was a certainty in the area at that time of year. The risks of both air and ground travel would be great, but if he could deliver the information to the Allies, the hazards were well worth it.

He would carry falsified papers giving him direct orders from Hitler's personal secretary, Martin Bormann. They were a mandate giving Jerry free course in Berlin to carry out specific details of Bormann's brainchild to purify the German race, producing what was referred to as the Aryan elite. The "Fountain of Life," predicted Bormann, would produce 10,000 purified children by the end of the war who would live in twenty-two homes administered by the society. The Nazis had already torn 200,000 children with Aryan characteristics from their parents in Norway, Poland, and Czechoslovakia to be raised as Germans.

It was late on the night of January 2, 1944. Jerry sat alone in the back of the four-engine Lancaster Bomber that the Resistance kept hidden in a large cave near Cherbourg. The Resistance had boarded up the entrance with authentic-looking signs saying that it was condemned and dangerous. They even placed loose rocks at the entrance that crumbled if any of the boards were moved.

The mile-long road leading to Cherbourg was perfectly straight for about a quarter of a mile, making an ideal runway, and the cloud cover hid the light from a full moon, so the takeoff was without event. Once in the air, Jerry went over and over his training instructions. It had been an intense time of jumping and landing, but the sheer volume of repetition had made jumping almost second nature to a point where his natural fears were under control. He checked his parachute one last time, and upon a signal from a member of the crew, he jumped into the darkness of the night and looked skyward to see the plane fly off into the distance. He was on his own.

The following day, a kindly farmer Jerry encountered agreed to drive him into Berlin. Jerry told him that his motorbike had had a blowout and lay crumpled in a ditch. The effects of his landing on rocky ground the night before —a large bruise on his right wrist and a cut on his forehead—seemed to authenticate his story in the man's mind.

That night, Jerry entered a bar and spotted an SS officer sitting alone. There was no way he could even remotely inquire about aircraft assembly plants without arousing suspicion, so he planned merely to make a friend and try to gauge the man's loyalties to the State. He had hoped that he would find someone who believed the Nazi cause was unjust.

He asked in German, "Mind if I sit here?"

The man didn't say a word but pushed a chair out with his foot so that Jerry could sit opposite him. The German was friendly, but even if he had been sympathetic to the Allied cause, there was little chance he would have let it be known. In the course of conversation he related that a week earlier, a soldier whose tongue had been loosened by a few beers had spoken too loudly. He casually mentioned that he considered something the Third Reich had done to be detrimental to Germany.

About an hour later, the SS showed up and escorted him away for questioning. At 11:00 a.m. the next day, he was taken to the main square and shot in public, his bullet-riddled body left tied to a post for two days as a warning to others not to resist the State. They wanted it to be known that if they didn't hesitate to shoot one of their own, they would gladly deal with others who refused to fall into line with their wishes.

After hearing that, Jerry decided that his only hope of finding someone willing to give him the information he needed would be in one of Berlin's ghettos.

As he stood later that evening at the checkpoint of the largest ghetto, an officer closely examined his papers and asked, "Why are you wanting to enter here?"

"We understand that a number of Norwegian children are being hidden by the Jews," Jerry answered with an air of authority. "I have come to make inquiries. I find that a little money here and there can loosen the tightest tongue, especially when the belly is empty."

The officer smiled, obviously impressed that the orders came directly from Bormann himself, and said, "To make sure you are not put in danger, I will provide you with an escort of two soldiers and my personal vehicle."

As Jerry was driven through the ghetto, he looked in horror at starving women whose husbands most likely had either been imprisoned in the nearby concentration camps or killed. The women were sitting on the sidewalks, or lying with their children, their emaciated faces and pleading eyes slowly following his car.

After driving around for about ten minutes, he told the driver to stop the vehicle, charged both soldiers to remain in the car, and walked over to a woman sitting on the cold sidewalk.

∽∘∾

RACHEL SLOWLY opened the door of what used to be one of many communal kitchens in that region of the ghetto. The wide-open mouths of the cupboards told their own pathetic story. They held nothing but piles of rat droppings. The flickering light of a candle had drawn her into the kitchen, giving her a faint hope that someone may have found food and could give her some...anything to stop the unending gnawing in the pit of her stomach.

But it was just old Rabbi Cohen, sitting at the large table reading the Bible in dim candlelight. She had often seen him shuffling around the ghetto, clutching his Bible like a child clutches a beloved rag doll. Disheartened, she slumped down on the floor in a corner. Another pain, greater than the hunger, gripped her heart. It was the memory of seeing her precious husband shot before her eyes by the Nazis, his body tossed onto a truck bed like refuse from the streets.

As the sun rose and made the candle unnecessary, the old rabbi lifted his eyes, licked his thumb and forefinger and squeezed out the flame. Rachel stared at the smoking wick, and thought of the black smoke that ascended continually from the Buchenwald concentration camp, where the Nazis were snuffing out her people.

As she looked at its smoke, she was distracted from her thoughts by the sound of a page being turned in the rabbi's book. She stared at him for fifteen minutes as he slowly and thoughtfully turned each of its pages with an obvious reverence. His eyes didn't look up for even a moment from its contents.

At last she broke the silence. "Why do you read that book?" There was a bitter cynicism in her tone.

Without looking up he merely answered, "It is my food."

The gnawing in her stomach made her annoyed at such a stupid statement, but before she could reply he continued, "Some people have a thousand questions. With this book I have a thousand answers."

"My mother used to read the Scriptures all the time," Rachel observed. "*She* went to Ravensbruck."

He still didn't look up, but just said, "Do you have questions, or answers?"

Rachel didn't reply as his words echoed in her mind.

After several minutes he lifted his eyes, adjusted his rimmed glasses on his nose, and looked over at her. "My dear, I warned our people that money had become our god. Oh, we didn't dance around a golden calf and take off our clothes as the children of Israel did when Moses was on the holy mount. But we may as well have, because we as a nation have forgotten our Creator. I showed them again and again that Israel fell into judgment when they forsook the Law and worshiped idols, but they wouldn't listen. We worship idols. Not wood and stone images, but idols of material wealth. Idols of the businesses of life ... and we give God lip-service. They retired this 'raving old Jeremiah.' But I warned them."

He could see that Rachel's expression was questioning, so he continued, "Listen to the book of Jeremiah, as the God of our fathers speaks to His people: 'How shall I pardon thee for this? thy children have forsaken me, and sworn by them that are no gods; when I had fed them to the full, they then committed adultery, and assembled themselves by troops in the harlots' houses. They were as fed horses in the morning: every one neighed after his neighbour's wife. Shall I not visit for these things? saith the LORD:

and shall not my soul be avenged on such a nation as this?'"

The old rabbi somberly added, "Then judgment came: 'Their widows are increased to me above the sand of the seas: I have brought upon them against the mother of the young men a spoiler at noonday: I have caused him to fall upon it suddenly, and terrors upon the city... and the residue of them will I deliver to the sword before their enemies, saith the LORD...They shall die grievous deaths; they shall not be lamented; neither shall they be buried; but they shall be as dung upon the face of the earth...'

"For years I warned our people that they could not love money, commit sexual sins, and forget the Law of their God. I told them that if they would not turn from their wickedness, He would judge us, to bring us back to Himself. I read them the words of Jeremiah: 'Give glory to the LORD your God, before he cause darkness, and before your feet stumble upon the dark mountains, and, while ye look for light, he turn it into the shadow of death, and make it gross darkness. But if ye will not hear it, my soul shall weep in secret places for your pride; and mine eye shall weep sore, and run down with tears, because the LORD's flock is carried away captive.'"

He looked up from the book and with tears streaming down his cheeks said, "My dear, our light has turned to gross darkness...but our God is rich in mercy to all who call upon Him. He will judge Germany, and once again cause His face to shine upon us. One day Messiah will come and restore all things. The God of our fathers will draw us back to Jerusalem. He who scattered Israel will gather her."

His naiveté angered her. Rachel glared at him and said, "I cannot accept your God. *He is a tyrant!*"

"*Hitler* is the tyrant," he responded. "Can't you see that you are doing what Israel did? You are creating your own god. Your image of God is not the one given to us in the Scriptures. Jeremiah has been labeled a 'prophet of doom,' but he was a prophet of *good* tidings. His very name means 'Jehovah will exalt.' God was willing, so willing to turn from His wrath and exalt His people by pouring His blessings on them, but they refused to turn from their rebellious ways. That was their choice. We, as His people, had that same choice."

"What *choice* is this? We are starving to death! I have no money, no food, no family." Glaring at the old man she argued, "I cannot believe that

God would just sit back and allow *this* to happen to 'His' people!"

Rabbi Cohen looked back at the Scriptures he had just read, and said, "My dear... He *has*."

As she stood to her feet enraged, he calmly added, "But I have not seen the righteous forsaken, or His children begging bread..."

With that she snapped, "You stay here and die. I am going to beg for bread!" and stormed out of the room slamming the door.

Her anger seemed to energize her as she scoured the streets of the ghetto looking for food. She was so angry at God and so desperate, she decided to sell her body to any man who would take her, but all she could find were widows and sickly, old men.

By this time she had become very weak with hunger. She returned to her section of the ghetto, crumbling onto the cold pavement near where she had left more than seven hours earlier. No one came to her rescue. In her weakness she felt a strange emotion, one that she hadn't felt for a long time. It was a sense of guilt. It wasn't for what she had done as much as it was guilt for what she had become. She was angry at God, angry at Rabbi Cohen, angry at what life had dealt her. The rabbi's words echoed in her mind.

Rachel *had* forgotten God...she had given Him only lip-service...Then there were other things, things that she knew were morally abhorrent to the holy One of Israel. She suddenly felt unclean and lifted her hands to her face, partly in despair and partly to hide herself from facing God. She slowly removed her hands from her face and faintly whispered, "Oh God of my fathers, the God of Abraham, Isaac, and Jacob, Jehovah-Jirah, Rabbi Cohen was right. I have sinned against You. I was going to sell my body. I am ashamed...I am so weak with hunger... help me..."

It was then that a shadow crossed her weary face, startling her. As she focused her eyes, to her horror she saw the tall figure of an SS officer. She cowered in fear as he knelt down beside her. Then he gently opened her hand and, to her disbelief, placed within it a roll of money. She was confused. Was he propositioning her?

He whispered, "Don't be afraid, and don't be fooled by the uniform. My name is Jeremiah Adamson. I am an American working with the French Resistance. *Please*...I must find out where the German aircraft plants are in Berlin."

Rachel listened to the tone of his voice and noted his earnest expression. She looked at the soldiers waiting in the car, then inquiringly back at Jerry.

"They think I am an officer of the SS on special assignment for the Führer, trying to uncover information about missing Norwegian children." Then he smiled slightly and said, "The Resistance can produce some fine German paperwork."

Again he said, "*Please*...it is vital to the Allied cause. Why would I lie to you? All I need are the locations. You may keep all the money; buy yourself something to eat."

Rachel was stunned by what had just taken place. Seconds earlier she had prayed to the God of Israel to provide for her! She thought for a moment, lifted her weak body to her feet and said, "Wait here," then disappeared around a corner.

Jerry walked back to the car. "I think I am onto something," he told the soldiers. "The woman has seen two children who don't look like Jews...a little money goes a long way in making a Jew talk." They smiled as he wandered back to the sidewalk.

The rabbi looked up in surprise as Rachel thrust open the kitchen door. He had fallen asleep with the Bible still open at the book of Jeremiah.

Her eyes, flashing with anger when she left, now sparkled with life as she waved the fistful of money before his startled face and blurted out, "The God of our fathers has not forsaken us! He heard my prayer!"

When she told him what had happened, he began to weep. "My dear, God be praised—this is truly wonderful!" he marveled. "I have the name of a man who could give this American all the information he needs. *But how can I be sure this is not a trap?* I could be signing this man's death warrant. What if this is just a Nazi scheme to—"

Rachel held up her hand to stop his words and said, "Rabbi, this man is from God. I forgot to tell you his name...it's *Jeremiah*."

∽◦∾

IT WAS JANUARY 20, 1944, as Jerry sat in his room back in Paris, feeling a deep sense of satisfaction for his role in finding key German installations. He reached out and fine-tuned an old radio as he listened to the BBC. It crackled:

"The RAF dropped 2,300 tons of bombs over Berlin today, just one week after a massive array of 1,400 American planes darkened the central German skies, unloading a barrage of bombs that obliterated three key Nazi aircraft assembly plants. Despite the loss of 59 heavy bombers and five fighter jets, the United States Eighth Air Force called its assault a 'major military success' and German dispatches even acknowledged that 'the enemy was technically superior.' The three plants that were hit were Oschersieben, Halberstadt, and Brunswick, all-important factories of war for the Third Reich. Virtually all available planes in the *Luftwaffe* arsenal (about 100) were used in defense. Of those, 28 were downed by American fighters."

CHAPTER SEVEN
THE SECRET ROOM

J ERRY'S NEWFOUND friend Charles was a typical French freedom fighter. He loved to sing, he loved wine, and he loved women even more. Most of all, he loved liberty. He had taken all these things for granted up until the German occupation. He lost his brother and father on the island of Corsica a year earlier in a bombing raid, and yet the tragedies that had come his way hadn't taken from him his love of life. Instead, they had hardened his resolve to fight oppression.

Soon after the first bombing raid that killed his father and brother, the Nazis arrived on the island in force. Charles had been torn between staying with the remaining members of his family or joining the Resistance. If he stayed in Corsica he risked being shot, so his mother and sister pleaded with him to leave the island and fight on the mainland for his country. He escaped the island in a fishing boat with three other men, and shortly after made contact with the Resistance.

Like many others, this gentle fisherman had been hardened to the realities of war through years of fighting. He had stabbed, shot, and poisoned Nazis, and even strangled them with his bare hands.

It wasn't long until the local Resistance began its work on Corsica. They saw their mandate as doing anything that would frustrate, confuse, or hinder the enemy—from cutting communication wires to carrying out full-scale attacks on convoys.

Charles had spoken often about his happy, carefree childhood, so it didn't surprise Jerry when he decided to return to the island. Charles said it was his prayer that when the Nazis began retreating, Corsica would be their first backward step. What was surprising was his insistence that Jerry go with him. It didn't take long for Jerry to make a decision. He quickly assembled the few belongings he would need. He then gathered Lillian's few possessions, put them in a box and gave them to their landlady for safekeeping, should Lillian return.

Thanks to Resistance expertise in travel documentation and a willing French fisherman and his sturdy vessel, the two men soon found themselves on the island of Corsica. Jerry felt as though he had already been there, especially after he was given a crash course of the island and its history during the one-hundred-mile boat trip. The birthplace of Napoleon, it was the fourth largest island in the Mediterranean and was strikingly beautiful. The island looked like a mountain range jutting out of the sea. It was covered with hills and steep mountains, except for the eastern side of the island, which was primarily a coastal plain. That's where they decided to land the fishing vessel.

The men quickly made contact with the local Resistance, who informed them that the Nazis had closed a vital link between two parts of the island. Their first mission was given to them shortly after their arrival: they were to take out a guard post not far from where they landed. They would have the invaluable help of two attractive female members of the Resistance who lived on that part of the island.

The four rehearsed their plan of attack. The women, Camile and Simone, would let the air out of the back tire of their car. They would also let down their hair and pull their blouses down over their shoulders to attract the guards. They told the men they hated doing this, because they were churchgoing women. One of them quoted the words of Solomon—something about a man being brought "to a piece of bread" by a "whorish woman." In other words, when a loose woman tempts a man, he has little or no resistance. They were counting on the truth of this verse.

Simone said that when her younger sister was raped by a German soldier, a Nazi doctor had aborted the pregnancy. It was a nightmare for her sister, and she would never be the same. Another friend, who refused to become a "call girl" for the soldiers, was raped and then shot through the head by the soldier who assaulted her. He claimed that she had tried to kill him and that it was self-defense. There was no official inquiry into the incident.

As the men waited in the bushes to execute their plan, Jerry's heart pounded as hard as when he had hidden under the bakery floor in Bialystok. He never found killing another human being to be easy. He had to become detached— like a killing machine. He dare not let his fear, or other emotions, let him think about what he was doing. He just did it. He did it for France. He did it for the free world...for his family.

Two armed guards sat casually in the outpost. One lit a cigarette and puffed on it in the cold night air. Just then there was the sound of a limping car coming around a corner. It was the women, precisely on time. As the car hobbled toward the outpost, the soldier put out his cigarette, took a firm hold of his rifle and cautiously approached the vehicle. Jerry heard him tell Camile to turn off the car lights. She immediately did so. He then directed the other guard to shine a spotlight into the car and then directly at the women. Both men liked what they saw. He then told them to get out of the car and to slowly walk toward them.

It was when Camile said something about giving the men a "good time" that both soldiers let their defenses down. It was only for a moment, but it was obvious that her words diffused the air of its tension. The men's body language changed. The weapons in their hands were no longer held high. That was all that was needed. Within seconds, both soldiers were seized from behind, had their throats slit, and their bodies quickly dragged into the bushes. It was fast, efficient, and professional.

~∞~

JERRY'S EYES BOGGLED at the array of weapons that the Resistance had amassed on the island. One of the leaders explained that the Allies had secretly armed them, and that what Jerry saw was only a small portion of a huge arsenal. As they drank wine in flickering candlelight, the local Resistance leader explained that the supply was kept hidden on a local farm. It had been there for years, and despite numerous searches, the Nazis had never found it. This was because of its ingenious location.

Jerry was told that in 1939, a man named Francois Berdau had built a secret room to hide his family from the Germans. He was a Frenchman by birth, but in 1915 he had moved to Berlin and set up a bookbinding business. In the mid 1920s he fell in love with and married a pretty Jewish girl named Ingrid.

Bonnier, the local Resistance leader, greatly admired Francois, not only because they were the best of friends before the occupation, but because of what he had been doing for the cause of France. During the evening, he gave Jerry the details of his friend's background.

Francois, who had majored in political studies at a Parisian university, was deeply fascinated with what was happening in the German political arena. In 1932 Adolf Hitler, the leader of the National Socialist Party, had gained an incredible 37 percent of the vote in a run-off election for the presidency of Germany. That meant that more than 13 million Germans wanted him as their leader, despite his radical ideas.

Hitler openly clashed with the existing German government because Chancellor von Papen refused to give the Nazi leader a Cabinet seat. Earlier, the then President of Germany refused Hitler's demand to be made a dictator. Hitler said that he could no longer tolerate the present government and that it would be only a matter of time until the Nazi Party gained total victory. Hitler promised to restore the economy and the dignity of the German people, and millions were swayed by his words.

What fascinated Francois was that Hitler's words were almost prophetic. On March 23, 1933, Adolf Hitler was granted virtual dictatorial powers.

As Francois continued to follow the political scene, he couldn't help becoming a little concerned. Hitler's newfound power meant that he could make laws by decree, without submitting them to the Reichstag. Nevertheless, Francois decided that he should attend a political rally and hear the charismatic leader himself.

As he entered the huge hall, the atmosphere was electric and very well organized. By the time Hitler made his entrance to the platform, there was an overwhelming sense of excitement in the air. Francois had never felt anything like it. Hitler was small in stature, but his words were full of power and hope, and the huge crowd showed their delight with roaring applause. It was as though there was a mysterious authority that came with each word. Even though he had gone there to formulate an impartial opinion, Francois found himself standing when the crowd stood. He applauded when they did. He joyfully shouted with the throng, and even saluted Hitler with them. He had never felt such soul-stirring enthusiasm for any other cause.

But when he heard Hitler proclaim, "Treason toward the nation and the people shall in the future be stamped out with ruthless barbarity," he stopped roaring with the crowd. He stood silently and soberly calmed himself. In a moment of time he drew on his political knowledge. Anyone who would use such words could only be a tyrant.

His concerns were heightened when billboards were placed around Berlin proclaiming "Jews the world over are trying to crash the new Germany." On May 10, a huge bonfire was lit in front of Berlin University and thousands of schoolchildren watched as books were burned. The same was done in Munich. The wide-eyed children who observed the spectacle were told that it was for the good of the Fatherland.

This horrified Francois. One of the main reasons he had chosen to be in the bookbinding business was because he loved the knowledge that books passed on to following generations. Among other things, books had the ability to show errors made in history, so that we could learn from them and not repeat the same mistakes. When he read the statement by Nazi Interior Minister Wilhelm Frick that schools must constantly emphasize that the infiltration of the German people with alien blood, especially Jewish and Negro, must be prevented, he began to seriously consider returning with his family to France. He told Ingrid to keep herself and the two children indoors as much as possible, while he inquired about the possibility of leaving.

Two months later Hitler's government announced a new program designed to weed out

Germans who were less than perfect. Doctors would sterilize them for the glory of the Reich. Under the new law, men and women would be sterilized if they were deemed to have a mental or physical "weakness." That clinched it for Francois. One of his children had polio, and the disease had left her physically weak. Very weak. Despite claims by the Nazis (under international pressure) that they would lessen the campaign against the Jews, Francois felt that for his family's sake, they must quickly leave his beloved Berlin.

Francois managed to sell his business to a German publishing company, gathered his earnings and his family, and took a fast train to Paris. They then traveled on to Corsica.

The day the small Berdau family left for France, they heard that terror had gripped the fashionable Kurfurstendamm district as a gang of two hundred angry Nazis viciously beat a group of Jews, screaming, "Destruction to Jews!" Any cooperation of Germans with Jews brought immediate punishment. Towns in the Cologne district forbade any Jews from settling there. Barbers were not even allowed to cut Jewish hair, and any who did so were arrested as "race defilers." If any Germans became romantically involved with Jews, both were arrested and sent to separate concentration camps—the males to Lichtenberg and the females to Moringen.

Once in Corsica, Francois was surprised how little the island had changed in the twenty or so years he had been gone. He showed his family where he used to go fishing, where he went hiking with friends, and he even showed them a tree house he had built. He smiled as he pointed out that it was still there...after all the years.

As soon as he purchased his farm on Corsica, he decided to build the secret room to hide his family should persecution spread throughout Europe. His fears were soon realized as he watched the conquering of the countries that surrounded Germany. One by one they fell, while the world passively watched.

Despite his provision, he never used the room to hide his family. When it became evident that the Germans would conquer France, he instead sent his wife and children to friends in Britain, deciding that his German citizenship and the fact that he spoke fluent German would ensure his safety. It did.

He met with the Resistance just before the occupation, and they decided that he should be publicly known as a German sympathizer but would secretly work with the French. This is why Bonnier so admired his friend, whom few of the locals knew was loyal to France. Because he was seen as a Nazi sympathizer, he was hated by the French and had even been severely beaten by a group of fishermen who viewed him as a traitor. Francois didn't let his true loyalties be known, however, and the beating actually worked in favor of the Resistance. From then on the Nazis completely trusted Francois, and he often hosted dinners for local Nazi leaders, lavishing them with wine, women, song, and the fatted pig.

This was one reason that the Germans never discovered the secret room filled with weapons. There was another reason—one that made both Francois and all who knew of its location quietly smile. The arsenal was hidden beneath Francois's pigsty, and the pigsty, of course, was always filthy. Piles of stinking waste covered the concrete floor, ensuring that the immediate area was never searched. Only once did the Nazis come close to finding the cache. In their efforts to uncover members of the local Resistance, they determined to thoroughly scour every inch of the island, including Francois's property.

They systematically explored all areas of the farm, except for a certain part of the floor of the pigsty. Two soldiers thrust their bayonets into a few piles of straw. They checked out the pig food, and crawled into the foul-smelling area where the pigs slept at night. They even tipped over a large water container, revealing nothing but a solid concrete floor.

Concrete also protruded out of the filth in two other places in the sty, giving the impression that the whole floor was rock-solid. And it was . . . except for one eighteen-inch-square, three-inch-thick concrete trap door that led to the huge arsenal of weapons. Francois had embedded a small hook, attached to a strong wire, in the concrete door. To access the secret room, he would locate the wire and pull it upward to lift the door. The opening was just big enough for the lean Frenchman to slip into and pass out weapons to thankful Resistance leaders.

CHAPTER EIGHT
THERE IS NO GOD

❦

ONE THING AFTER another fueled Jerry's burning rage against the Nazis, and it was taking its toll. A number of Frenchmen had been fighting alongside the Germans. Called the "Legion of French Volunteers Against Bolshevism," they gathered at the famed Velodrome in Paris, waving French flags while wearing German uniforms. Their only complaint was that the Germans weren't giving them enough to do. They were tired of simply watching roads and railway stations. They wanted to hunt down the Resistance and those they called "terrorists."

Jerry considered these men to be cowardly traitors. There were German sympathizers in every country, but these scum were standing on the blood of their own people. Where was their respect for the sacrifice that their own countrymen had made? He was appalled by what they were doing, and it made him feel that the fight in France was futile. It was as if the whole world was insane. Frenchmen fighting for Germany —fighting alongside those who humiliated and slaughtered their own people. Jerry decided that he would retreat to Britain. He needed to think, to consolidate, and the thought of the courage of the British and the fact that they still held their island consoled him.

His plan was to travel discreetly through Vichy France, the unoccupied southern "free zone," then once in Paris it would be just a matter of a relatively short hop across the English Channel to Britain. His contacts with the Resistance would help to get him through. As he traveled north, he encountered the small village of Oradour-sur-Glane, which was remarkably free from the concentration of soldiers that were in Paris. Struck by its peacefulness, he decided to take a break from the war and enjoy the quieter country life.

As the days went by, the villagers that he met welcomed him with open arms and made him feel part of their families, often inviting him to their homes for a meal. One young girl he met was a soft-spoken teen named Monique, whose passion to liberate France from the Germans reminded him of Lillian. She had a sweet innocence and a deep passion for life. After staying in Oradour for several weeks, Jerry found himself thinking increasingly of his own family. Monique was such a reflection of Lillian that it rekindled a spark of hope that his sister was still alive—somewhere. With a renewed sense of purpose, he decided to continue on to Paris, to search again for news of Lillian, before heading on to Britain.

Once he arrived in Paris, he met with his friends from the Resistance so they could fill each other in with what had been happening. Upon hearing that he had been staying in Oradour, two Resistance members looked soberly at each other and then back at Jerry. They informed him that they had just received reliable information that the Germans had killed every person they could find in the tiny village. To his horror, he learned that a total of 642 people had been rounded up and slaughtered—the entire village massacred. The Nazis were avenging the capture of an SS officer by the Resistance, and an unconfirmed rumor said he had been executed in Oradour.

A witness explained that the SS encircled the village, dividing the men into five or six groups and herding them into barns. The women and children were locked in the church building. The men were shot first, then the church was set on fire. Any women and children who tried to escape were shot dead. At 6:00 that evening the Germans stopped a train and shot all those who were heading for Oradour.

News of this sickened Jerry beyond words. It was as though the bitterness of life had struck a deathblow to his very soul. He withdrew into a deep anger both at the Nazis and at God, who had allowed them to cause such suffering.

Reprisal massacres such as this were not unusual for the Nazis. Jerry heard that recently in Rome the Gestapo had indiscriminately rounded up 335 people—including two Italian priests, a number of Jews, some women, and two teenage boys—and mercilessly shot them to death. They were killed in reprisal for a bomb attack that had slain thirty-three German policemen. Hitler had demanded that within twenty-four hours fifty Italians be executed for each German who died, but officials in Italy reduced the ratio. Hitler's cold-bloodedness in these atrocities was truly chilling.

∽∘∾

With no further news of Lillian's whereabouts, Jerry, disheartened, picked up the box of possessions he had left with their former landlady. Seeing Lillian's belongings again brought tears to his eyes. Among them was a Bible—the one that his father had read from as he prayed that Britain and France would deliver his family from the Nazis. "Some help that was!" Jerry muttered as tears streamed down his cheeks. He threw it back in the box and spat out, "There is no God!"

That conclusion seemed to justify his anger. What "prayers" had God answered? Where was this God when his beloved father was shot? If He knew where Lillian was or what had happened to her, He certainly didn't bother to tell Jerry. The very thought of an all-loving Divine Being made him bitter. Besides, he had seen "God with us" engraved on the belt buckles of the Nazi soldiers. Even the demented Führer believed in God! A year earlier, Jerry had come across portions of Hitler's *Mein Kampf*. When the First World War began and lifted Hitler from obscurity, he recorded in his book how the war made him elated, saying, "I fell on my knees and thanked Heaven from an overflowing heart."

Jerry's newfound atheism gave him some sort of solace and explanation for the sufferings he saw around him. If there was an omnipotent God, how could He sit idly by and watch Lillian and Jean suffer? How could a "God of love" let his family members, Monique's entire village, and countless women and children be so brutally murdered? And of all things, how could He do nothing while the Nazis were slaughtering millions of Jews, His "chosen people"?

Aside from the horrible plight of women and children he had witnessed in the ghetto in Berlin, tales of ghastly incidents had trickled back from the concentration camps with such detail he couldn't help believing them. He kept hearing stories of innocent children being used by "doctors" as guinea pigs in amputations, and in tests of lethal germs and toxins. Polish and Soviet officials estimated that 1.5 million people were put to death at the Majdanek concentration camp. The camp covered 670 acres and was surrounded by an electric barbed fence and protected by fourteen machine-gun turrets.

The victims were Jews and Christians—men, women, and children from every nation in Europe—and were processed very efficiently. The prisoners were first herded into bathhouses and stripped, their clothing sent to Germany to supplement the German wardrobe. They were then moved into another room that was sealed except for holes high in the roof, from which canisters of a toxic gas were dropped. The warm showers the people took opened their pores, permitting the gas to take effect more quickly. Prison guards watched through glass panes in the ceiling to make sure everyone had been killed.

The dead were removed, and their gold teeth and fillings were knocked out and later sold. Bodies were then taken to a furnace and burned in ten to twelve minutes, meaning that when the crematoriums were efficiently used, 1,900 bodies could be burned a day. *The ashes were then sold to German farmers as fertilizer.*

No... there was no God.

CHAPTER NINE

CRAWLING WITH GERMANS

❧

J ERRY PICKED UP his only possessions after
nearly four years of working with the Resistance. In addition to his beloved sister's torn
Bible, he had his father's .38, which he had used
to kill two SS officers, and a few items of clothing that he carried in a small brown leather
suitcase. He had accomplished the sweetest of
victories in Berlin, but he had seen too many
terrible things for a young man his age. Jerry
desperately wanted to get out of France and
leave behind his painful past.

He had abandoned his American papers
after the U.S. entered the war, and instead traveled under French papers given to him by the
Resistance. They arranged for him to be picked
up and transported by car from Paris to the
small fishing village of Port en Bessin. There a

fishing boat would take him across the English Channel to Newhaven, where he would be met and taken to the British Foreign Office in London, fifty miles to the north.

As he and two members of the Resistance, Pierre and Jacques, set out on a crisp and clear night of June 4, it should have been a simple thing for the three "fishermen" to return to their village after selling their catch in Paris. But they had a growing uneasiness as they neared the coast. The remote area of the countryside was crawling with Germans. They passed battalion after battalion and trucks towing 20mm guns.

"I am *from* Port en Bessin," Jacques said nervously, "and I have never seen it like this!" Thousands of soldiers were being transported and the checkpoints became more and more frequent.

The men grew silent as they approached the lights of what was normally a quiet fishing village. "I don't like this," Pierre said.

Jerry felt the same. "Why don't we pull over to the side of the road?"

Pierre didn't hesitate. He swung the car to the edge of the road and turned off its lights.

The three men sat in the dark and stared at the commotion ahead of them. They could hear the rumbling of tanks and trucks and see the silhouettes of artillery being driven through the tiny village.

"The invasion...they *must* have details of the invasion!" whispered Jerry. British intelligence had informed the Resistance on June 1, via a coded message on the BBC, of the Allies' invasion of France. However, because Jerry had withdrawn earlier from active work with the Resistance, he had not been privy to the particulars.

The men decided that it would be too risky to drive into the village or to try to return to Paris that night. The Germans wouldn't want French fishermen rising up at their backs while the Allies were attacking at the front. There was no doubt that they would have either imprisoned or shot the locals. The three decided to travel by foot through the fields to the outskirts of the village and try to get details on what was going on.

They crouched behind a small rowboat and listened to the sound of German voices coming from the kitchen of a fisherman's modest home. They were about 500 yards from the center of the village near the cliffs overlooking the English Channel. The roar of the waves on the still, cold night and the rumble of distant trucks made it difficult to hear what the voices were saying.

Suddenly the three men crouched low as the front door of the house swung open and an SS officer stood on the porch. He looked around thoughtfully, then up to the clear sky and took a deep breath. Then he put his hand into his pocket and pulled out a flat silver case, slowly opened it as though his mind was elsewhere, took out a cigarette and hit the end of it against the palm of his left hand.

When he put the cigarette into his mouth and lit it, Jacques grabbed the binoculars that hung around his neck and slowly lifted them to his eyes. From the uniform he could see that this was "top brass"—a general. As the glow from the cigarette lighter illuminated the man's face Jacques whispered, "It's Carl von Schlieben!"

After smoking only half of the cigarette, the infamous general dropped it onto the wooden planks and ground it out with his foot as though he had suddenly thought of something important, and strode back into the house.

Jacques longed to get closer, but the place was alive with activity, and two soldiers stood guard at the entrance. Pierre took hold of the binoculars and moved to one side so that he could see through a window, almost choking Jacques as he did so with the strap that was still around his neck. Jacques smiled as he lifted it over his head.

The general was leaning over something on the table in front of him. From what Pierre could tell, standing around him were two other generals and four or five top SS officers. When one moved to the side he could see that they were looking at a map spread out on the table. It was obvious, with such an elite gathering, that this was the defensive strategy for the Allied invasion.

"From the information we have, and by the look of what's happening here," Pierre whispered, "I would say the Allies will land in this area either tomorrow or the next day, on June 6." Jerry found out later that this was known as "D-Day." The term "D-Day" was the date on which operations began. The day before D-Day was known as "D-1," while the day after D-Day was "D+1." This meant that if the projected date of an operation changed, all the dates in the plan did not also need to be changed. This was the case with the Normandy landings. The Allied landing was originally intended to be on June 5, 1944, but at the last minute bad weather delayed it until the following day.

Pierre knew the area well and said that if it was where the Allies had chosen to land troops, they would be sitting ducks under the artillery on the cliffs. The men decided to wait until morning and see in the light of day the extent of the German military.

During the night, the three men made their way to a high area about two miles along the coast. From there they would be able to see the cliffs overlooking the Baie de la Seine.

As the sun rose, they peered in amazement at the scene before them. As far as the eye could see, there were masses of German high-powered artillery set back from the edges of the cliffs. On the cliff edges were bunkers, each containing two soldiers with machineguns.

As Jacques surveyed the incredible sight of so many guns and men, he broke the silence. "Dear God, if they land on this beach, they will be slaughtered."

During the hours of that day, the men remained in the thicket on the cliffs, straining their eyes toward the horizon, planning what they would do. They decided to wait until nightfall and get as close as they could to the bunker at the northern end of the cliffs. That position was strategic as it was a little higher than the rest of the area.

It was 6:00 a.m. the next day. Without taking his eyes away from the small binoculars in his hand, Pierre suddenly prodded his two companions awake and said, "There they are!"

Jerry rubbed the sleep from his eyes, took hold of the glasses and uttered, "Look at that sight..." It truly was an awesome spectacle. It was still dark but the entire horizon, aglow with the rising sun, served as a backdrop for the blackened silhouettes of 5,000 battleships—*Allied* battleships. Jerry stared at the sight. This was the trumpet-blowing cavalry coming for the remnant of fighting soldiers. *It was a realization of the prayers of millions in war-torn Europe.*

Little did he know that the majority of the troops who landed on the D-Day beaches were from the United Kingdom, Canada, and the U.S. but that there were also courageous soldiers from Australia, Belgium, Czechoslovakia, France, Greece, the Netherlands, New Zealand, Norway, and Poland.

There was no time to spare. The three men quickly blackened their faces with charcoal and scurried down the hillside toward the first bunker. They knew that every German eye would be toward the horizon. With the glow of the pre-dawn sun, they could see the outline of two men sitting beside a large machinegun. One had his hand readied on top of the weapon and his eyes on the horizon. The other was also staring silently in the same direction, as steam rose from the coffee in his right hand. In the cold hush of the morning the three Resistance fighters silently slid down into the bunker. Either the Germans thought it was their friends joining them in the bunker, or they were so intent on the enemy in front of them that they didn't hear the enemy behind them. It was almost too easy as the three men cupped their hands over the mouths of the Germans, forced them to the ground and quickly slid sharp knives across their throats. They pulled them to one side, stripped them of their jackets and helmets, then Pierre and Jerry put them on and took hold of the machinegun. The next outpost was a mere sixty feet away, but the operation had been so quiet they hadn't aroused any suspicion.

Jacques was a cool character. He picked up a mug from the dirt and poured coffee from a flask in front of him. Then he sipped it as he drank in the sight on the horizon. Jerry smiled and gently patted the weapon as if he was patting a dog that was pulling at the leash, wanting to attack its prey.

When the morning light spread across the beach below them, they could see tens of thousands of German machine-gunners, as far as the eye could see, lying in the sand behind tufts of grass. As the Allied forces approached the shores, the horizon darkened as the skies filled with air support. When the roar of the planes became louder, a German voice came over the radio that was lying in the soil of the bunker. "You have your orders," the voice crackled. "May God be with you." That made Jerry fume.

Suddenly, there was a massive boom of artillery as the 450mm guns behind them blazed against the Allies and signaled the machine-guns to open fire on the troops pouring onto the beach. Jerry immediately turned the gun to the left and discharged a mass of bullets into the bunker less than twenty yards away. Then he lifted his sights and did the same with the one next to it. Then he swung the firearm toward the hordes of German soldiers lying on the beach below him and rained bullets onto them as Pierre fed the hungry gun its fill of ammunition.

The sight of so many Allied soldiers being hit by the torrent of German bullets was too much for Jacques. Masses of them were being killed before they even had a chance to reach the shore. Their dead and wounded bodies floated among the blood-crimson foam of the waves. These were men who were giving their lives to liberate France.

With total disregard for the fact that he would be seen by rows of German artillery stationed 100 feet back from the cliff, Jacques climbed out of the shelter of the bunker. He then ran across to the bunker containing two dead Germans and pushed their bodies aside. In the heat of battle, he picked up two machine-guns and with one in each hand, ran to the back of the third bunker of stunned Germans who didn't expect to be attacked from behind, filling them with lead. Then he hurtled himself into it and began firing like a madman at everything that moved. It was a suicide mission. Predictably, there was a sudden explosion right on top of Jacques' bunker, as the Germans put an end to the life of this courageous Frenchman.

On that one special day, the Allies landed around 156,000 troops in Normandy. The American forces landed a total of 73,000: approximately 23,000 on Utah Beach, 34,000 on Omaha Beach, and 16,000 airborne troops. In the British and Canadian sector, 83,000 were landed (62,000 of them British): 25,000 on Gold Beach,

21,000 on Juno Beach, 29,000 on Sword Beach, and 8,000 airborne troops. A massive total of almost 12,000 aircraft were available to support the landings.

Approximately 2,700 British, 1,000 Canadians, and 6,600 American soldiers were killed. The total German casualties on D-Day are not known, but are estimated to be between 4,000 and 9,000 men.

CHAPTER TEN
LIBERATION!

∾◦∾

L ONDON WAS in ruins. Hitler had terrorized the residents with his "miracle weapon"— the V-1. The pilotless, jet-propelled bomber carried more than a ton of explosives and flew at a speed of 370 mph. After one raid, Winston Churchill had the unenviable task of announcing to Parliament that the weapon had taken 2,752 British lives. However, the great statesman was confident that Germany would never conquer Britain.

In a broadcast via the BBC to the French, Churchill declared, "We are waiting for the long-promised invasion. So are the fishes."

A short time after the V-1 attacks, despite the massive loss of life on the beachfront, the Allies drove back the Germans from the shores of Normandy and took out the launching pads for the V-1 rockets. The battles had raged from June 6 through June 27, and at times the German defense seemed almost invincible. They had stationed a row of four "pillboxes," which stopped the Allies in their tracks.

Finally at the end of June, soldiers were able to advance close enough to destroy them by tossing grenades through their ventilators. The two freedom fighters joined themselves to Allied forces and discovered a tunnel in the southern quarter of Cherbourg. When smoke from Nazi gunfire spewed out, the Americans decided that they would blast the tunnel open.

Just at that moment, a private emerged holding onto a white flag. He informed one of the American commanders that General Carl von Schlieben was within the tunnel and wished to surrender. Jerry watched in delight as 800 soldiers proceeded to emerge from the tunnel. A total of 30,000 German soldiers surrendered to the Allies at Cherbourg.

Even as the Allies advanced across Europe, Hitler continued bombarding London using V-2 rockets. These carried the same amount of explosives as the V-1, but they were faster and deadlier. They traveled at the speed of sound and it was almost impossible to detect their approach.

Before taking his leave of France, Jerry decided to backtrack with the Allies to enjoy the sweetness of taking Paris back from the Germans. The liberation began on August 25, 1944, when General Charles de Gaulle led a tumultuous parade through the streets of Paris, and that night church bells rang all over the city.

Jerry's long trip to England had been uneventful. Even the boat ride across the English Channel was an unusually smooth one, for which he was thankful. Despite the devastation Jerry found in London, he liked being in England. The British made a "Yank" feel special.

After the war ended he decided he would try to recapture his lost youth. He had just turned twenty-one and as far as he could see, he had two options. He could either return to Texas and join his mother on the farm, or he could begin a new life in England.

He had reestablished contact with his mother and she was doing fine. The friend his father had left managing the farm had been able to get it on its feet financially, and it was drawing a healthy wage for both himself and Jerry's mom. So, he decided that he would try living in England and if it didn't work out, he would return to the U.S.

After he had made his decision to stay, he applied for a job with a government construction company in London. There was no shortage of work, as London had to be rebuilt. It was physically hard work but the pay was good, and because he lived very simply, he was able to save most of his paycheck. It wasn't long before he had his own car and had moved to a better apartment in Wembley, on the outskirts of London.

Friends at work would often encourage Jerry to join them for darts at a local pub. It was at the pub that he met Connie, a quiet young woman with a strong Yorkshire accent. One day, he noticed that she was watching his every move as he played darts with a friend, so he offered to buy her a drink. She accepted and it wasn't long before they had established a friendship.

Connie was petite, very pretty, had warm brown eyes, blondish curly hair, and a typical light British complexion. At the outbreak of the war, when she was fourteen years old, her parents moved her from London to the small town of Otley to live with an aunt for safekeeping. Both her parents were killed in the bombing raids and their bodies were never recovered. The first time Jerry and Connie sat together and ate fish and chips, he asked her about her past and she wept openly as she spoke of her folks. There were a lot of tears in London.

Jerry fell deeply in love with this soft-spoken young lady. He loved everything about her, including her strong accent. She was different from the outgoing girls he had met in France. Though she was very reserved, she was sincere and kind, with a sweetness that made him want to be near her. Some may have seen her as a wallflower, but every flower on close examination was a thing of great beauty. But there was something else that endeared Jerry to her: because of the loss of her parents, he felt a deep empathy toward her. When he put a comforting arm around her as she wept, it made him feel good. It uncovered a tenderness he had forgotten that he possessed. He loved the fact that she listened to him when he spoke, and he would often catch her staring at him for no reason as they ate lunch together. After six months of a close friendship they became engaged, and eight months later they were married in a small Anglican church not too far from Jerry's apartment.

CHAPTER ELEVEN
A Faithful Friend

❧

WHEN CONNIE'S aunt became ill with tuberculosis, they moved to Otley to care for her. Two months later she tragically died, and left her cottage to Connie. The couple sold the property and with the proceeds, together with a bank loan, they purchased a sheep farm just north of Otley.

Jerry loved the green countryside. Parts of it reminded him of France, especially around the Oradour-sur-Glane district. The two of them would arise in the cool of each morning at six o'clock and begin the many duties around the farm. They had two dogs that helped round up the sheep. One was a pure-bred border collie they named Faithful, because of the character of the breed; the other, Sam, was a mixed breed rescued from the local pound. Both dogs were instinctive when it came to rounding up sheep, but Faithful was particularly intelligent.

Connie and Jerry loved walking together to the barn and unleashing the dogs first thing in the morning. The animals would yelp with excitement, wag their tails, and almost choke themselves as they pulled at the ropes that restrained them. As soon as they were released, Faithful would run around in circles of delight at the prospect of getting onto the back of the truck. Both dogs would stand right on the edge of the flatbed and lean into the wind, their eyes scouring the horizon of the fields as though they had never seen the countryside before.

Rarely did the Adamsons leave the farm. They saved every penny from the sale of wool, and occasionally meat, and the vegetables they grew in their rich soil. The local farmer's market wasn't just a way to get income, but it was also a way to meet people from the town. With that extra money, they purchased a small herd of milking cows, and milking became a twice-daily occurrence. Even if one of them went into Otley for supplies, it was never for more than half a day.

In December 1945, Connie returned from a routine visit to the doctor. Her face glowed as she drove the flatbed and parked it by the barn. Jerry came out of the barn holding a shovel in his hand, and as he opened the truck door he asked, "Well, what's the verdict?"

Beaming from ear to ear, she said in her broad accent, "Doctor says there's a bun in the oven. You are going to be a father!"

Jerry was stunned. He had never thought of himself as a father. He had known so much death and suffering and now he was going to be given a life. His reaction was different from Connie's big smile. He was so overcome that tears suddenly welled in his eyes, and he cupped his hands over his mouth to hold back his emotions. Connie knew how he felt. She stepped forward to hug him, and immediately his sobs became joyful intermingled with the occasional "Wow!"

A couple of months later, as Connie emerged from a checkup at the clinic, she encountered an old school friend. During her school years she had had a crush on him and even dated him briefly, but she was surprised that in such a short time he had changed. A desk job at the local newspaper, coupled with good home cooking, had given him a pot belly. Connie smiled as she thought that she must look the same to him, but her belly wasn't the result of lack of exercise.

As they stood by her truck, he quizzed her on what she had been doing since the war. She took a few minutes to fill him in on her new life. When she let slip that Jerry had been with the French Resistance for four years, he raised his eyebrows and said, "I would love to do a story about you two; nothing sensational, just a local human interest story. What do you say?" Connie knew that Jerry didn't like to boast about the war, so she smiled and said she would talk it over with him, and they agreed that he would phone her the next day.

Two weeks later, a half-page article appeared in the local newspaper. Jerry had reluctantly agreed to the story, as long as the reporter put emphasis on the fact that he was an American who had married a local girl, and not too much on the war. He wanted to downplay the fact that he had been a freedom fighter for the Resistance. Jerry didn't see himself as some sort of war hero. To him the real heroes were men like Jacques and the Allied soldiers who lay dead on the beaches of Normandy.

The couple laughed together as they read about themselves, with a large photo of the two of them clad in farm attire, standing next to their beloved dogs, grinning back at them from the page. Connie's old flame kept his word. The only mention of the war was a small bit of alliteration, with which the reporter couldn't help finishing his article. It merely said, "The Adamsons love their life in Otley, especially American-born Mr. Adamson, who says frankly that he finds farming a far cry from when he fought fearlessly for four years for the French freedom fighters." That made them laugh even more.

There was now another mouth to feed on the "famous" farm: a beautiful seven-pound baby boy named Johnny. His arrival changed their lives radically. No longer did they go out together in the cool of the early morning to the barn to release the dogs, and trips in the truck entailed only Jerry and the two wagging tails. The baby had to be taken care of and that was something they both accepted gladly. Four months later, Connie was pregnant again, and they were thrilled to welcome a girl, Elizabeth, to the family that summer.

The change in their lifestyle was the main reason Jerry took on a hired hand. When Bill Lovock showed up at the farm one day looking for work, Jerry hired him on the spot. He was a good worker but he kept to himself. That didn't worry Jerry too much because he liked the private seclusion of his own lifestyle with his family.

Bill did, however, open up when it came to one subject—the war—but those conversations were one-sided. The "discussions" were more Bill giving his opinion rather than the two of them discussing anything. The man seemed to have some sort of resentment toward Winston Churchill, which wasn't unheard of. Some were jealous of his political success, and Jerry dismissed Bill's attitude as "to each his own."

About a week after the new worker was hired, they received a call from the Adamsons' accountant in Texas. It wasn't unusual to get mail from the States, but it was uncommon to get a long-distance call. Jerry's mother often wrote and told him what was going on in his native country and her letters were always encouraging and informative. But Connie watched his face turn pale as he listened to the Texas drawl on the other end of the line.

The man gently explained that he had some very sad news. Mrs. Adamson had been tragically killed in a head-on collision with a cattle truck while returning from Dallas late the previous night. After surveying the scene and finding no skid marks, the police concluded that she had fallen asleep at the wheel of her pickup. The other driver had been treated at the hospital and released. Vance, the accountant, insisted that there was no need to return to the U.S., and that he would arrange the funeral and send him details on the farm's financial status.

CHAPTER TWELVE
HEAT OF THE NAKED FLAMES

S ITTING IN THE von Ludendorff's home in
Poland, Jerry's eyes widened as he listened
with rapt attention to Mr. von Ludendorff's
question. Even though the preacher was speaking to a congregation, it was as though Jerry
were on the only one in the room: "What is this
mystery of Christ? Have you discovered it yet?
Thank God I did when I was a young man."
Then Mr. von Ludendorff's eyes looked directly
at him as he inquired again, "What is the mystery of Christ? Do *you* know?"

There was a loud banging on the door. Nazis!
Jerry could hardly breathe. Fear gripped him as
he sat in the room staring at an orange glow
behind the preacher's head. Fire! *The Nazis were
setting the house on fire!* The confusion was mul-
tiplied by the excited barking of a dog. Jerry

began to cough violently. Mr. von Ludendorff stood amid the confusion and yelled, "Awake thou that sleepest, and *arise from the dead and Christ shall give thee light!*" The dog's barking became louder and louder.

Suddenly, Jerry awoke from his dream to the terrifying nightmare, coughing in his smoke-filled bedroom. *The house was on fire!* That part was no dream! Connie lay unconscious next to him. He quickly pulled her from the bed onto the floor. Many times during the war he had crawled through smoke-filled rooms and he knew that breathable air would be trapped close to the floor. *Johnny and Elizabeth!* They lay in their beds in the next room. He quickly crawled down the hallway and reached up to feel the door. It was cool, so he thrust it open. Their room was also full of smoke. He held his breath, stood to his feet, grabbed the children and crawled back to his wife. As he did so, he could hear the incessant barking of one of the dogs.

As Jerry pulled his beloved wife and children out into the fresh air on the front lawn, he could feel the heat of naked flames as they licked through the windows behind him like a huge monster reaching to devour its prey. He rolled Connie onto her stomach, put her limp arms under her head and began to press firmly on her back. Suddenly, she began to cough and show signs of life. Jerry whispered, "Thank God!"

He turned his attention to his two children beside him. Johnny, just five years old, was now conscious, revived in the fresh air, but he looked terrified—his face was white and he was shaking with fear. But by the light from the flames Jerry could see that Elizabeth had stopped breathing and had turned a ghostly blue. In a panic he grabbed her tiny lifeless body, turned her over and with both hands pressed on her back again and again. Tears streamed down his face as he prayed, "Please, God. *Please* let her live! Oh, God, don't let this child die. I'll do anything You want. *Please!*"

He kept pressing for what seemed like an eternity, but it was no use. Elizabeth wasn't responding. He picked her up and with trembling hands held her close to his chest and began to weep uncontrollably.

Suddenly, he felt a touch on his shoulder. He looked around, then down at Connie. She was still lying on the cold ground, but breathing normally. He looked behind him again. It was bizarre. *No one was there.* His child lay lifeless in his arms, yet the fear had gone, replaced with that same unmistakable peace he once felt when he entered the von Ludendorff's home so long ago.

Then Jerry heard the most wonderful sound. A tiny gagging noise came from his little girl! Tears poured from his eyes, this time for a different reason. He squeezed Elizabeth tightly in his arms, looked to the heavens and whispered, "Thank you, God. Thank you, God!"

Quite a statement—for an atheist.

CHAPTER THIRTEEN
NOT IN THE UNITED STATES

∽∘∾

THE ADAMSONS moved into their neighbor's home at their invitation, and took their dogs with them. The night of the fire, Faithful had chewed through his rope when he saw the flames through the open door of the barn, then he stood beneath the bedroom window and barked his sweet little canine heart out. The house was in ruins but the family was intact, and that was all that mattered to them.

The local police investigated the fire and determined that it had been deliberately set. That was no surprise to Jerry. After their hired hand had suddenly disappeared the night of the fire, it didn't take Sherlock Homes to put two and two together. Despite their investigation, Jerry didn't have much confidence in the Otley Police Department; it wasn't exactly Scotland Yard.

There were only three full-time officers, and the typical crime in the area was a stolen bicycle —and even that was infrequent. That's why he was amazed to hear Inspector Simmons explain that Mr. "Bill Lovock" wasn't who he claimed to be. His real name was Wilhelm Schmidt, a German citizen who came to Britain with his parents in 1936. The parents returned to Germany in 1939 at the outbreak of the war and the father joined the SS. They left their teenage son in Britain as an informant, thinking that because he was young he wouldn't be a suspect and could be useful to the cause of the Party.

"The man is a Nazi through and through," the inspector explained. "He is very bitter that Hitler's dream to rule the world has failed. Schmidt hated Jews, blacks, and anyone who stood against the Party. We have been tracking him for years, but he kept slipping through our fingers. Then he would suddenly show up in different areas of the country and set fire to things. In the past it has been churches and government buildings. He must have seen the article about you in the paper. We will get him soon.

"By the way, Mr. Adamson," he added, "in the course of the investigation we took a number of items away the morning after the fire.

One of them was a .38 pistol. I know you don't have the weapon for unlawful purposes, but this is not the United States. One of my men mentioned that you have been considering moving back there, so we will keep it down at the station until that time. Normally, we wouldn't return a weapon to its owner; but we are grateful for the work you have done for Britain, so you can pick it up when and if you decide to leave the country."

It was while the Adamson family was still staying with the neighbors that Jerry received another call from the United States. Hearing Vance's rich Texas accent brought back memories of their last conversation, and he braced himself for more bad news.

The accountant began by thanking him for returning the release form he'd sent earlier in the year. Jerry didn't know what he was talking about, so he excused himself, covered the mouthpiece with his hand and asked Connie, "Did I sign a form earlier—something about a release for an oil company to survey on Mom's farm?"

Connie nodded. "You signed it along with about a hundred bills you paid in March," she said. "You may not remember because I mailed it."

He lifted the phone back to his mouth and said, "Sorry about that, Vance; carry on." The accountant explained that the company's prospecting had just been routine, but that he now had some good news for the Adamson family.

"The whole area of surrounding farmland is oil-rich. *They struck oil on your property this morning at 9:35!* Jerry-boy, you had better mosey on home. You and your wife are rich. Very rich!"

CHAPTER FOURTEEN
WHO IS LUCIANO?

〰️

IT WAS MAY 1962. As Jerry sat in the living room of his plush Texas home in Royse City, he flipped through an English newspaper sent to him by an old friend in Otley, and casually glanced over the music section. A new group, with what was being called a "Mersey beat," was finding big success back in Liverpool, England. Jerry wasn't at all interested in modern music, but any news about Great Britain always caught his interest.

He smiled at the thought of Liverpool. Many times he and Connie had driven there and sat in the cold wooden stands, enjoying cups of warm coffee and an even warmer crowd, to cheer on their favorite soccer team. He lowered the paper to his lap and licked his lips as he recalled the delicious English fish and chips with salt and vinegar, grinning that just the thought of them made his mouth water.

He continued reading the article, which identified the new group as The Beatles. Decca, a major British recording studio, had rejected them, saying, "We don't like their sound. Groups of guitars are on the way out."

Jerry glanced across to the other page as he mumbled, "Well, they should know what—"

A heading on the opposite page arrested his attention and stopped him mid-thought: "Israel Hangs Eichmann for Death Camp Acts." His hands began to shake as he read the piece: "Inside a fog-enshrouded Israeli prison, a noose was place around the neck of Adolf Eichmann just before midnight last night. His final appeal for mercy had been rejected. Eichmann's ankles and knees were tied. He said a few last words and then a black trap door sprang open in the floor. Eichmann, the man who sent millions of Jews to their deaths in Nazi concentration camps, was dead.

"'Long live Germany, long live Argentina, long live Austria,' Eichmann said just before he was executed.

"'But to sum it all up,' wrote Eichmann in his memoirs, 'I must say that I regret nothing

...Hitler was somehow so supremely capable that the people recognized him. And so with that ...I recognize him joyfully and I still defend him. I will not humble myself or repent in any way...No, I must say truthfully that if we had killed all the 10 million Jews that statisticians originally listed in 1933, I would say, 'Good, we have destroyed an enemy.'

"Argentina was the country where he hid until he was kidnapped by Israeli security agents. 'I had to obey the rules of war and my flag. I am ready,' were the mass murderer's final words. In denying Eichmann's appeal for mercy, the Israeli Supreme Court said he had shown no repentance for his crimes. It was reported that he had committed them with 'genuine joy and enthusiasm.' The Justices also called the death sentence 'inadequate compared to the millions of deaths in the most diverse ways he had inflicted on his victims.'"

By the time Jerry finished the article, beads of sweat had formed on his brow and his jaw was clenched. His hands were knotted in fists so tight that his knuckles were drained of blood. In his mind he tried to imagine Eichmann's eyes bulging with terror as he hung by the rope. It sickened him that the mass murderer's pain was so short-lived. He wanted desperately to believe that there was a God and a burning Hell that awaited him and every other Nazi who had ever breathed this earth's air into his evil lungs.

He remembered the limited feeling of satisfaction after he so closely followed the Nuremberg trials back in 1946, which resulted in nine of Hitler's henchmen swinging from the end of a rope. It was almost anti-climatic when they were hung. It didn't stop the pain of losing his father and sister, his grandmother and Joseph, or the countless friends who died fighting the malignant cancer of the Nazis. Today's newspaper item only stirred the demons of hatred, bitterness, and anger within him. All he wanted to do was forget the past, but the past would not forget him. Every memory brought with it other recollections that carried unbearable pain.

Vance was right. Oil had made Jerry very rich. Money dripped from the affluent fingers of the Adamson family. Everything Jerry touched turned to gold. What's more, everyone liked him. Why wouldn't they? He became a giver of fine gifts—big gifts: cars, boats, and money. Lots of money. The Royse City authorities also liked him because he was very philanthropic. Generosity was his middle name. Oil had made him millions, but he had shrewdly transferred his wealth into stocks and bonds, which greatly increased his fortune. He was a risk-taker in war and in peace, and his financial risk-taking efforts were rewarded with huge dividends.

Jeremiah P. Adamson was no longer the simple-living farmer he had been in England. Money does strange things to people, and over the years affluence changed him into a man of the world. He had become someone who epitomized Shakespeare's warning to "flee ambition, for by such sin fell the angels."

Amid the sea of wealth, Connie and Jerry had drifted apart and virtually lived two separate lives in their own home. Jerry's life was consumed with running his business and taking care of his money, and Connie's life was devoted to Johnny and Elizabeth, now in their mid-teens.

Although his name was a household word in the district, the public wasn't aware that many of his business dealings had created adversaries. The business world is a hard and steep climb, and often one has to tread on a few fingers to get there. After death threats started, bodyguards followed Jerry almost everywhere he went.

There were also more than a few large and shady financial dealings with people the police had been investigating, but the investigations never came too close to Jerry, thanks to friends in high places.

Jerry appeared to be a warm and generous man, but beneath the exterior of benevolence, money had surfaced another side to him that was seen only by those who were closest to him. His war experiences and his business dealings made him into a cold, ruthless businessman. In time, he degenerated to a point where he gave gifts only because it created friends who would do whatever he wanted. Money gave him power over people, and power gave him pleasure.

Little did anyone but his accountant know that he had another dirty little secret. Years previously, he had invested almost all of his wealth into a very high-yielding overseas fund, which had recently crashed overnight, sending him wildly into debt. But late one night, he and Vance met with some overseas bankers and secured a massive loan against casino properties he owned in Las Vegas. The casinos were not paying their way, and day by day Jerry was sinking into a giant whirlpool of liability. Once a month, he would meet secretly with his creditors and plead for an extension of his loans, each time assuring them that the casinos would begin turning a profit.

At one of these meetings, his creditors advised him that they wanted to balance their books and that he had until the end of the month to meet interest payments. If he was unable to do so they would take radical action to "secure their investment."

After that meeting, Jerry took steps to acquire more credit through large city banks, but each time he was turned down, something he wasn't used to. This added more fuel to his simmering anger. His call to his accountant was laced with expletives. "Vance, I don't care what you have to do, *but get me some credit somewhere!*" With his neck veins bulging he screamed, "I don't care how much interest you have to pay, or where you have to go to get it, but get it. *Now!*" Click!

In a last-ditch effort, he secured a huge loan from a foreign bank and embarked on a two-million-dollar television advertising blitz to promote his casinos. He also made public the fact that he had low-risk, high-yielding bonds, and vast quantities of revenue poured in from trusting investors. But instead of investing the money into bonds, he secretly used it for advertisements. He hoped to pay it back when the campaign roused the casinos from their slumber. But the advertising campaign was a disaster. Much to his horror the economy suddenly went sour and people held onto their dollars with a tight fist, sucking him even further and further into his mammoth whirlpool.

To try to keep his head above water, he mortgaged everything he still owned outside of his business. This included his home, his yacht, and one of his two luxury cars, to yield liquid cash needed to remain in the extravagant lifestyle he so loved. He wouldn't face reality. Jeremiah P. Adamson was living in a dream world, thinking that somehow he would never have to balance the books.

The sale of his assets, along with a large short-term, high-interest loan Vance secured through a private corporation in Florida, eased the pressure from his creditors. However, in time the stress began to take its toll on Jerry. This once happy man became deeply depressed and began drinking copious amounts of alcohol just to make it through each day. His dream world turned into a nightmare. The parties, the admirers, the compliments didn't do for him what they once did. It was evident to his close friends that something was drastically wrong. His creditors' phone calls became frequent and heated. His fast lane had become a dead end.

One evening there was a knock at the door. Instead of opening it, Jerry sat in the living room with a drink in his hand, hoping whoever it was would go away.

Suddenly, there was loud crash as the door was kicked in. Three large, well-dressed men stood directly in front of a quickly sobered-up, wide-eyed Jerry. The spokesman said calmly, "You should have opened the door, Jerry. My boss won't be too pleased to hear that we had to break it down just to speak to you." He grinned and added, "We had hoped this would be a pleasant visit."

"Who are you and what do you want?" demanded Jerry. The man smiled again, calmly inhaled his cigarette and said, "My name isn't important. My boss is Mr. Luciano, a name with which you are evidently not familiar. You should be; you owe him a great deal of money. We hear through the grapevine that you are in a hole."

A forced smile revealing his yellowing teeth, the man reached up and picked a photo off the shelf, and stubbed his burning cigarette into the face of Elizabeth, Jerry's beloved daughter. "My boss doesn't like to hear that people who owe him money can't pay up," he said, his smile disappearing. "It would be sad if something happened to your kid. You have one week to settle things with Mr. Luciano. I understand your accountant knows how to contact him."

At that, the three men left, leaving Jerry stunned. He quickly picked up the phone, called Vance and asked, *"Who the blazes is this guy Luciano!?"*

Vance was quiet for a moment. "I didn't know until this afternoon," he said. "I'm sorry, Jerry. When I got you that loan from a corporation, I thought they were legit. He's a cousin of 'Lucky' Luciano, who, back in 1936, was sent to prison for twenty-five years for running a $12-million-a-year prostitution ring in New York City.

"I had no idea that this guy in Florida was a bigwig in the Mafia."

CHAPTER FIFTEEN
GLIMMER OF LIGHT

❦

THE VISIT FROM the Mob scared Jerry. *Really* scared him. It brought back fears reminiscent of Nazi Germany. For three days he soaked himself in alcohol from the time he got up until the time he fell into bed. As he pondered his dilemma, he began to contemplate the unthinkable: suicide.

On the morning of the fourth day there was a knock of a different sort at his door. It was the law with a warrant for his arrest. His overseas creditors had begun the proceedings they warned him about.

This once rich, happy, proud, and generous benefactor was about to be arrested and—no doubt with much publicity—humiliated and dragged to prison like a common criminal.

As the two officers stood in his doorway, Jerry desperately searched his mind for someone, *anyone*, who may be able to help him. The banks had pulled tight their purse strings and he now owned nothing of material value with which he could negotiate. The situation was utterly hopeless. His heart sank into even deeper despondency. What was happening didn't seem real.

Suddenly, he remembered a man named Theodore Lawson, who lived near the property where he first struck oil. This neighbor was exceptionally wealthy, but there were terrible ill feelings between them, mainly because he frowned on Jerry's continual flirtations. One night years earlier when the two couples were gathered for dinner at the Adamsons', Jerry showed up drunk and greatly insulted Grace, Theodore's wife. Although she had always seemed very kind and virtuous, Jerry cornered her away from their spouses and made an unwanted advance toward her. She naturally told her husband about the incident. When Theodore confronted him about his low moral ethics, Jerry told him in no uncertain terms that his life was none of his business, and had had him physically thrown off his property. The two had been at odds ever since.

But Jerry knew that Theodore was a religious man, and there was a chance he would forgive him for what he had done. Perhaps he would lend him the money he needed to get the law off his back and rescue him out of his terrible nightmare. In light of the way Jerry had treated him, it would be very humbling to ask, but it was his last and only hope. He obtained permission from the officers to make one call. He slowly lifted the phone and dialed the number.

When Grace answered the phone, Jerry nervously said, "May I please speak to Theodore?"

She immediately recognized his voice and warmly answered, "Jerry, why don't you come in person and see us? Theo has spoken often of you. He has closely followed everything you have been doing."

Jerry couldn't believe what he was hearing. It was amazing that Grace remembered him and that her husband had actually shown an interest in his activities. Putting down the phone, he walked over to the law officers and pleaded that they allow him to visit his old neighbor. When he explained that there was a chance he could raise some of the money to pay his creditors, they agreed to escort him, explaining that if he tried to escape he would find himself in deep trouble.

He sat quietly in the back of the police car, grateful that the law had at least allowed him to follow this last glimmer of light down the very straight and narrow road to Theodore's house.

As he knocked on the large door, it opened to reveal Grace in all her innocent beauty. She looked deeply into Jerry's weary eyes, reached out compassionately and took him by his hand. It was as though she knew what he had come for. Then she gently took him into Theodore's study.

As Jerry entered the lavish room, he felt overwhelmingly wretched. The last time they had looked at each other was when Jerry cursed him to his face. Theodore sat at a large oak desk. His clear eyes seemed to look right into Jerry's heart, but it wasn't a look of condescension. It was one of warm welcome. All Jerry could think of was the way he had insulted and ridiculed this truly good man. Theodore had always done business with the utmost integrity, something Jerry had scorned. As he sat down in front of the desk he could hardly lift his head. He took a deep breath and said quietly, "I have come for your help…"

When he confessed what he had done and that he was greatly in debt, Theodore asked for the exact amount of liability he had incurred, including the loan from the Mafia. The total was in excess of twenty million dollars, but if Theodore could lend him even half of that, it would give him some respite. Without hesitation, Theodore called for Grace, gave her a key and whispered into her ear.

A few moments later, she reappeared holding a check. Jerry thought her hand was trembling as she gave it to him. He whispered, "Thank you," then glanced down at the amount. He couldn't believe what he saw. *The check was for the entire amount of the debt!* He didn't expect them to lend him *anything*, let alone the full amount. He had an idea what these people were worth and knew that this check represented their *entire* fortune. This display of kindness was utterly undeserved. He felt deeply humbled, and at the same time unspeakably grateful. This payment represented his very life.

The loan would mean that he wouldn't be publicly humiliated and thrown into prison. It would mean that the Mafia would leave him alone, and that he could stand up once again and look his friends in the eye. The loan meant that suicide was no longer an option.

He looked into the eyes of the man he once despised and thought of as his enemy and said,

"You had every right not to lend me this money and to throw me off your property."

Theodore smiled. "Oh, Jeremiah, it's not a loan," he said. "It's a gift."

CHAPTER SIXTEEN
I Need a Favor

❧

THE SIGHT WAS **momentous.** More than 200,000 peaceful participants filled Washington to demand the passage of civil rights legislation. It was an evening in August 1963, and Jerry watched on television as the Rev. Dr. Martin Luther King Jr. spoke to a great throng standing before him. His voice resonated with inspiring conviction.

After the news that night the only words that remained in Jerry's mind were, "I have a dream." His mind flashed back to Otley the night of the fire so long ago, to the dream he'd had that was so vivid. He had often thought about it, and the consequences had he not been awakened by the barking of his dog.

Suddenly, his thoughts were broken by the sound of a truck pulling up the driveway. Moments later, a key turned in the door and Johnny entered the living room. He seemed a bit distant but cordial, somewhat different from the last time the two had exchanged words.

As Johnny reached his teenage years, the relationship between him and his father changed. It was as though the dad he always looked up to had suddenly become "uncool." They rarely communicated anymore, and when they did, tempers often flared and the conversation would invariably end in shouting. Then his mother became concerned about the type of company he was keeping, and asked Jerry if he could somehow mention it to the boy. Much to Jerry's sorrow, the conversation escalated into a full-blown argument, at the height of which Johnny contested, "What about you and your friends during the war? Some of them weren't the 'best of company,' and while we are on the subject, I'm sick and tired of hearing you talk about 'back then.'"

By now he was yelling at his father. As he walked toward the door he turned and spat out, "The days of glory are gone, Dad! All you have from them are some faded medals. I'm getting out of here before I end up an old man with nothing but faded memories!" With that, he walked out and slammed the door.

Jerry knew he was right about the medals. There was a strange irony about the war. He contended that he hated it, but at the same time he missed the glory of living for what he believed was a just cause. The medals given to him by the French government were faded, and the "days of glory" had, over the years, become just a pale memory.

The following day, Johnny called and told his mom that he had gotten an apartment in Dallas. In addition to the very generous "allowance" he and his sister were given, they each had a savings fund for college—which Johnny quickly raided. Now he could finally live the way he wanted to live.

Like his dad as a teen, Johnny looked older than his age. His tall, solid build, handsome square jaw, deep voice, and the fact that he sometimes had to shave twice a day helped him easily pass for an adult. Besides, he had become a convincing liar. So he didn't have any trouble renting an apartment or finding work. Now, more than three months after the blowup, he had shown up at home like everything was just fine.

"Did you see the news tonight—the protest at Washington?" he casually asked. "Incredible, huh?"

Putting the vivid memories of their last exchange out of his mind, Jerry rubbed his forehead, then his eyes, yawned and thoughtfully said, "Something big is stirring in the nation. That man King is a born leader. He reminds me of a man I knew in the, ah..." He stopped before he finished the sentence.

Johnny walked into the kitchen and helped himself to a bottle of Coke. "Yeah, Dad," he called as he took off the cap, "I need to ask you a favor."

Jerry sighed and as Johnny entered the room he asked, "How much do you want?" He didn't know that the college fund intended for Johnny's future had been accessed—and squandered.

"A few hundred dollars should do it. Thanks, Dad," Johnny said. Once the cash was stuffed in his pocket he added, "Also, I've been concerned lately about the violence in Dallas. I think I need a gun."

Jerry was suddenly no longer tired. Trying not to betray his surprise, he calmly inquired, "What do you want a gun for?"

The subject was material begging for another blowup. It seemed odd that his son entered the room talking about a peaceful protest in Washington, and in the next breath he said he wanted a gun.

As the young man sat in front of him sipping his Coke, Jerry asked, "Are you in trouble?"

Johnny looked him in the eyes and said, "Dad, I don't want to clash with you on this. I need a gun *for protection*. I'm not in trouble, and I'm not going to do anything illegal, but I feel defenseless when I'm in Dallas at night. You know what it's been like recently with the increase in violence. You have the shotgun; how about letting me borrow Granddad's .38? I promise I'll take care of it."

When Jerry had left England he made sure that he picked up the gun from the Otley police station. Johnny had grown up with guns and knew how to handle them, but still it didn't seem right. "No, son. I've seen far too much death and bloodshed in the war," Jerry said. "You don't need to be thinking about shooting anyone, even in self-defense. If you're living in a dangerous neighborhood, you need to move back home where it's safe."

"Dad, the war is over, and you need to get over it!" Johnny exploded. "This isn't the 1940s in Nazi Germany anymore. It's the 1960s in America, and crime is a reality. If you won't give me the gun, I'm just going to take it!" With that he stormed into the room where the gun was kept, and he grabbed his grandfather's .38 and a box of ammunition.

As Johnny swung around, he paused just briefly with the barrel pointing toward his dad as if to say, You gonna stop me? "If you don't trust me, we're through!" he yelled. Then he disappeared out the front door, leaving his father speechless.

Johnny did need the gun. Not only was his apartment in an area of town that often erupted in violence, but he frequented a nightclub that had a few rough visitors. He didn't want any of them to make unwanted visits, and the gun would give him a sense of security. The nightclub, Ruby's, was actually a strip-joint, but Johnny maintained that he went there more to meet people. "Good conversation," he said. Once again, his rugged looks, plus a sob story that he had recently lost his driver's license when his wallet had been stolen, had convinced the nightclub manager to issue him a pass. Johnny was a smooth-talking liar, so people tended to believe anything he said.

The apartment was convenient in that it was only two miles from the newspaper where he worked. It also meant that he and his girlfriend, Darlene, could be alone. Darlene worked at the nightclub and she wasn't the sort of girl one would want to take home to meet Mom and Dad. She introduced him to Jack, the owner of the club. Mr. Ruby was a quiet man, about five foot seven with a receding hairline. He was originally a "hustler" from Chicago who liked to wear his black-banded hat everywhere he went. She also introduced Johnny to a whole new world: the world of drugs. At first he refused to have anything to do with the scene, but one day she convinced him to try a new "psychedelic" drug called LSD. A week earlier he had watched her for three hours on a "trip," as she raved about its mind-opening qualities. When she showed him a newspaper article where a number of respected doctors actually recommended it for therapy, he succumbed.

It wasn't long before Johnny found himself taking more and more LSD, and during that time there was a subtle change in his personality. It truly was a "mind-altering" drug—turning a bright outward personality inward. He also found himself in direct contact with drug dealers who sold more than "acid." They were forever encouraging him to try "smack," the ultimate "rush." Johnny vowed that he had too much self-respect to put a needle into his body, but as time passed LSD changed him even more. He found that without it, life was dull—so dull it became depressing. It didn't occur to him that the drug was causing his depression. Rather, he saw it as the cure.

It was during one of his times of despondency that he decided to head down to the club during the day, rather than go to work.

The door was partly open, so he walked in to find a man he knew who talked with a lisp. It was because of his lisp that his friends called him "Lips." Lips was a pusher, who, by the way he dressed, was obviously successful in his profession. When he saw Johnny open the door he stood to his feet and said, "Hey, Johnny, good to sthee you. What are you doing here at thith time of day?"

Johnny managed a smile. "I got sick of work," he said. "It's boring. Besides, my cash is a little low and I can't afford any acid."

Lips smiled warmly and said, "Hey, man, what are you doing on that junk anyway? I told you, you gotta give sthmack a chanth. It'th the ultimate buzth, I'm not lying to ya."

Johnny didn't reply. He just sat and listened as the salesman did his thing.

"I'll tell you what. I will give you sthome at no costht." Lips reached into his jacket pocket, pulled out a small folded piece of white paper and an outfit wrapped in plastic, set it on the table and walked off.

CHAPTER SEVENTEEN
RISK-FREE TERRITORY

A MONTH HAD passed since Johnny put the first shot of heroin into his arm. In those four weeks he had been fired from his job, but he soon secured another one with higher pay. This one was selling heroin.

After his first hit, he found his friend Lips, and spent every penny he had on more heroin, then raised money for the next week's supply by making another visit to his dad. He borrowed five hundred dollars by lying about needing to fix his car. But after their latest blowup, getting anything more from his father was no longer an option. When his money ran out he became involved in something he never thought he would stoop to: robbery.

He picked up his grandfather's short-barreled .38 and drove to a suburb of Dallas.

It was late at night. No one was around as he peered into a liquor store. Johnny sat in a darkened corner of the parking lot for over an hour watching an Asian man undo boxes, and then stack cigarettes and other items onto the shelves. At one point, there were no customers for more than forty minutes.

Johnny decided that he would wait until midnight then rob the store. His hands were shaking as he checked the gun to make sure it was loaded. He flipped the safety off, opened the car door, got out and cased the area. *Not a soul in sight.* He tucked the gun into his belt and partially zipped up his black leather jacket. Even though he felt terrified at what he was about to do, there was a sense of excitement, both in the robbery itself and in the fact that by morning he would have enough smack in his hands to last him a month.

As he quietly pushed open the door, the man behind the counter greeted him, then continued stacking his shelves. Johnny nodded and walked to the back of the store as though he were looking for something specific.

Moments later he burst toward the clerk holding the .38 in both hands. "I don't want to hurt you!" he yelled. "I need money now! Give me everything in the register and I promise you won't be harmed!"

The frightened man moved quickly and gave him everything in the cash register, then, without being told to, put his trembling hands in the air.

"If you move from here," Johnny threatened, "I will have to come back and shoot you!" As he ran toward the door, he stopped, turned toward the paralyzed man and added, "I'm sorry..."

He felt physically sick as he drove home, partly because he was beginning to withdraw from the heroin, and partly because he couldn't get the image of the man's terrified eyes out of his mind.

When he arrived at his apartment, he eagerly pulled the wad of bills from his pocket to total his cash. His heart sank as he found that they were mostly one-dollar bills with an occasional five, two tens, and a twenty. Everything he had gone through that night yielded a mere eighty-six dollars.

The next day, Johnny sold his almost new truck for about a quarter of its worth. When that money was gone, he stole a car from a parking lot three blocks from his apartment and sold it the same night to someone at the club.

After Lips discovered that he had hot-wired an auto, he enlightened Johnny on ways to raise cash without so much risk. It was far easier and less perilous to unload electronic goods through the nightclub, he advised, rather than a stolen car. One of the best times he had found to lift goods was on Sunday mornings. He smiled as he noted, "Almost every houth ith empty becauth people are at church!"

When Lips needed cash for his own habit, he would carry a bunch of fake circulars in his hand and go door to door. It was easy to check if anyone was home. He said that many religious people didn't even bother to lock their doors, so he would just go right on in and grab any cash and valuables that were small enough to hide under his jacket.

But Lips had a better suggestion for Johnny. He could work for him, selling smack. It was real simple, he said, and the money was good enough to support his habit and give him a very comfortable life. What's more, Lips would trust him with credit on the first shipment, *and* give him his own risk-free territory. Johnny could take over the college district, where there were no worries about undercover narcotic agents. It was an easy market. All he had to do was befriend some prospective buyers by showing them a little porn to gain their trust, then give them their first hit free...and they will be back for more. He laughed and said, "It'th sthoooo good to be able to have that thort of confidenth in your product!"

A couple of weeks later, Darlene walked up to Johnny as he sat at the club. She normally would have come up behind him and rubbed his shoulders or stroked his hair, but this night she simply called him over to a corner table.

"What's wrong?" he asked as he sat down opposite her. "I haven't seen you for almost three weeks." Whenever he had tried to get together with her, she was always too busy. He suspected something was going on, but he wasn't sure what it was.

Frowning, she blurted, "I'm pregnant. I need six hundred dollars quickly. If I don't get rid of this, Jack will fire me."

Johnny was stunned. It was the last thing he expected to hear. He also didn't like her attitude. "Get rid of this"? As far as he was concerned, "this" was a child she was talking about—their child—and there was no way he was going to pay for her to abort it. He reached out to put his hand on hers and gently said, "Darlene, I care about you. And I care about our kid."

Darlene winced as though she had just been slapped. She pulled her hand from under his as she said more loudly, "Don't be stupid. I told you, Jack won't like this!" She then rose from the table and began to walk away. Johnny stood to his feet, touched her shoulder, and pleaded, "Darlene…" She turned and glared at him like a cornered cat that was about to scratch his eyes out, and walked off leaving him speechless.

When Johnny returned to his apartment later that night, the door was unlocked. Darlene was the only other person with a key, so he hoped that she had changed her mind about the abortion and was waiting for him inside. But as he walked through the small apartment, he found that she wasn't there. Neither was the new stereo he had lined up for sale the following day. He rushed to his bedroom and opened the drawer where she knew he kept his cash. The four hundred dollars he had left there was gone. So was his .38.

In the drawer was a scribbled note saying simply "You owe me!"

The next day Johnny woke up wishing he hadn't. Not only did he feel nauseated, but he also felt frustrated and helpless. Darlene was going to have an abortion and there was nothing he could do about it. He was the father, and the child's mother hadn't consulted him about this decision. He couldn't shake the images he had seen of newborn babies. Before this, life to Johnny had simply been a matter of selfish pleasure, but now he was thinking about someone else: his child. His own child was going to have its life taken, and the thought sickened him.

He pulled the covers back, sat on the edge of his bed and stared at the calendar on the wall. It was November 22, 1963. His handwriting reminded him that today was the day he had to collect two hundred dollars from one of his customers and give half of it to Lips. Even though he had slept in his clothes and didn't need to dress, he could hardly gather the enthusiasm to do anything. He rolled back into bed and went back to sleep.

Around eleven he woke up and fumbled with a pack of cigarettes on his nightstand. His fingers trembled as he struck a match, then he took a deep breath of smoke. He exhaled loudly as he picked up a notebook he kept by his bed. In it were a few addresses and about a dozen depressing poems he had written about life. One was penned a few days earlier after a deal fell through and he began to withdraw. The poem, titled "Heroin," had just seemed to flow from his pen.

Shortly after noon he got out of bed, walked into his living room and turned on his huge old television—obviously too heavy for Darlene to steal. Then he plodded into the kitchen to make a strong pot of coffee.

He never finished making that pot. From the kitchen he heard words that sent shivers down his spine.

"*President Kennedy has been shot!* I repeat, the President of the United States has been shot."

Johnny rushed to the living room hoping it was some sort of sick joke and perched on the edge of his old couch in front of the TV.

Reporting from in front of Parkland Memorial Hospital, the newsman announced, "Just after noon shots were fired at the President's motorcade as it drove through the streets of Dallas." The reporter paused for a moment and looked slightly to one side. He began again, "I have just been—" His voice cracked with emotion. He composed himself and continued, "I have just been informed that President John F. Kennedy has been pronounced dead. He was killed today, just after noon by an assassin's bullet. It happened as he was being driven through

Dallas to the sound of cheering crowds. Suddenly, shots rang out and stunned the masses as the forty-six-year-old president crumpled in the seat of an open limousine.

"We have also been informed that Governor John B. Connally Jr. of Texas, who was riding in the same car as the Kennedys, was severely wounded in the chest, ribs, and arm."

Johnny sat glued to the television for the rest of the day as the media kept the public informed about the assassination. Some time later, they reported that police had arrested Lee Harvey Oswald and charged him with the murder.

The happenings of that day had Johnny in a daze. He didn't eat, he didn't drink, and neither did he give any thought to his heroin habit. That night he walked slowly to the bathroom and looked into the mirror. The assassination had had a sobering effect on him, confronting him with the transient nature of this life. One moment a man was smiling and waving at crowds, and the next moment he was dead! It was then that he remembered something he had once heard: that life is just a dash between two dates on a headstone.

He stared into the mirror at his unshaven face. He was still in his teens and yet he looked like an old man. His cheeks were sunken from poor nutrition, and his eyes looked like road maps, with dark circles under them. He whispered, "What am I doing with my life!"

Deep in thought, he walked back to his bedroom and picked up his open notebook from the bed, and began to read the poem he had written only days before. But as he read it, it was as though he could hear a sinister voice speaking to him through it. The voice said:

Behold my friend! I am heroin,
Known by all as destroyer of men.
From whence I came no one knows,
A far-off land where the poppy grows.

I came to this country without getting caught,
And since that day I've been hunted and sought.
Whole nations have gathered to plot my
    destruction,
They call me the breeder of crime and corruption.

More potent than whisky, more deadly than wine,
Yes I am the scourge of all mankind!
My little white grains are nothing but waste,
I'm soft and fluffy—but bitter to taste.

I'm white, I'm brown, but deadly to use,
For once you're addicted, I really abuse.

I'm known in China, Iraq and Iran,
I'm welcome in Turkey and I've been to Japan.

In cellophane bags I make my way,
To men in office and children at play,
From heads of state to lowliest bum,
From richest estate to lowliest slum.

I take a rich man and make him poor,
Take a maiden and make her a whore,
Make a beautiful woman forget her looks,
And make the student forget his books.

I can make you steal, borrow and beg,
Then search for a vein in your arm or your leg.
I'm known to the selfish and those filled with greed,
All faceless regardless of religion or creed.

My gift is illusion, my blessing is fake,
Death and destruction follow in my wake.
I'm the kiss of death to all who I touch,
I start as a gift and remain as a crutch.

My friends are many but I'm loyal to none,
I come to destroy and my work must be done.
Some think of me as merely a toy,
But wise men know I maim and destroy.

Run from me if you wish—I will never give chase,
For sooner or later you'll return for your taste.

Once in your bloodstream you'll think me not
    mean,
You'll praise me as master, then nod in a dream.

You've heard my warning but will take no heed.
Put your foot in the stirrup—mount this great
    steed,
Get right in the saddle and hold on real well,
For the white horse "heroin" will take you to Hell.[1]

∽∘∾

A THIN-FACED but clean-shaven young man
stood at the opened door of his parents' house
a little north of Royse City. This time he didn't
just walk in. Johnny looked at his beloved
mother standing by the door and his father
peering over the newspaper in his hands. Looking his father in the eyes he said, "Dad, I would
like to come home... *if you will have me.*"

Jerry was stunned. He put the paper down,
stood to his feet, and did something he hadn't
done in years—embraced his son, something
Johnny wouldn't allow once he became a teen.
Jerry was overcome at the thought of his wayward son coming home. He smiled warmly and
said, "Welcome home, son. We love you more

---

1 Similar to the song "King Heroin" by James Brown (based on a
  poem by Manny Rosen), the source of this version is unknown.

than you know. I can't tell you how happy we are to have you back as part of the family again."

Johnny poured his heart out to his parents. He confessed that he hadn't just experimented with drugs but had been using the most deadly of illegal drugs, and had committed robbery to support his habit. He shared how he had lost his job, become a drug dealer, and gotten his girlfriend pregnant, and he wept as he told how his girlfriend had killed their child by having an abortion. With tears streaming down his cheeks he turned to his father and said, "Dad, I also feel bad that Granddad's gun was stolen. You've had it since before the war, and I know how much it meant to you."

Smiling, Jerry assured him, "Son, that gun means nothing to compared to you. It doesn't matter what you've done—you are back home safe and that's all that's important."

The next evening Johnny's mouth dropped open as he and his family sat in the living room. Once again, he couldn't believe what he had just seen on television. Lee Harvey Oswald, the man accused of assassinating the President, had been shot to death that morning, and a camera-man caught the incident on film. Johnny leaned forward to stare at the slow-motion replay...at the man with the gun and the black-rimmed hat. "*I know that man.* That's Jack Ruby! He is the owner of the nightclub where—"

Johnny stopped mid-sentence as the newscaster provided details about the incident. The Dallas strip-club owner had simply walked down a ramp with fifty reporters and shot and killed Lee Harvey Oswald as he was being transferred by police to a bullet-proof van.

Then the news anchor intoned, "Using a snub-nosed .38, Ruby fired a shot that pierced Oswald's left side."

CHAPTER EIGHTEEN
EDUCATED MAN

∽◦∾

THE INCREDIBLE gift from Theodore Lawson was a godsend, allowing Jerry to pay off all his creditors and get back on his feet financially. Over the next several years, the economy improved and the casino business picked up. Life for Jeremiah P. Adamson became sweet once again. His relationship with Connie even improved a little, but he never confided in her about the depth of their financial trouble. Nor did she ever find out about the Mob's little visit. Still, even with what they had been through, the marriage lacked the closeness it once had.

That was one of the reasons Jerry found it easier to travel on business trips. Back in Otley he hated leaving Connie even to go into town for half a day, but now the trips gave him more of a chance to appreciate life and meet other people—especially intelligent, pretty women with colorful personalities. These encounters always began the same way. There would be talk on a variety of subjects, followed by an intimate meal at an exclusive restaurant, perhaps a gift, before ending up at a luxurious hotel. These were just one-night stands...no harm done. It was respectable prostitution.

One night after returning from a business trip to Vegas, he had a nightmare that began with him and his father running out the back door as Nazis fired shots at them. This time, however, instead of running ahead when his father was shot, he stopped and picked him up. Then he found himself once again in the von Ludendorff's home with the penetrating eyes of the preacher staring at him. Again he kept hearing the question reverberate, "Do *you* know the mystery of Christ?"

Then the preacher glared at Jerry and said, "Adulterers will not inherit the kingdom of God!" Jerry tried to hide behind the person in front of him, but the preacher stepped to one side and, pointing directly at him, said again, "Adulterers God will judge."

Jerry stood to his feet and cried out, "No... I'm sorry!"

But the preacher took no notice. "Please…," Jerry began to weep, "I'm sorry for what I have done!"

Just then he felt someone touch his shoulder, and he heard a soothing English voice say, "It's okay, honey—you're having a nightmare."

Jerry sat up in bed, looked at Connie, and then glanced around him as though he didn't believe her. Sweat was dripping from his brow and his bedclothes were soaking wet. He looked down at his hands that were shaking even though he was now wide awake. He could feel his heart pounding in his chest and his breathing labored as if he had just run up a flight of stairs.

Seeing the fear on his face Connie said, "That must have been *some* nightmare."

"I don't know what's happening to me," Jerry said, looking straight ahead. "I have had horrible dreams about the war, but they have never been like this. With this one I keep ending up at the von Ludendorff's house." He turned to face Connie, and with an expression of wide-eyed helplessness told her about the dream, minus the verse about adultery. The next night he dreamed again that he was at the Bible study. This time the preacher said, "Murderers will not inherit the kingdom of God."

Jerry stood to his feet and said, "I am not a murderer. I only killed in the war."

But the preacher looked at him with a piercing gaze and said, "God knows how many people you killed when you could have let them go. You hated them, and the Bible says that hatred is murder of the heart. *You are no different from the Nazis!*"

Again Jerry began mumbling incoherently in his sleep and awoke dripping with sweat. As before, Connie soothed his fears and held his hand until the fear subsided. It was in those times that he felt a glimmer of the feelings he had had for her in the early days of their marriage.

One afternoon Connie returned from the doctor looking quite pale. A few weeks earlier she had discovered a lump in her left breast and went to have it checked out, then went back to learn the test results.

Suddenly Jerry was the one holding *her* hand as she told him the lump was malignant. As gently as the doctor could, he had informed her that it was inoperable and that, even with the best of treatments, she had a maximum of six months to live. Jerry held her in his arms as they both wept. The thought of losing her ripped his very heart out and rekindled his love for her.

He had been taking his wife for granted, and determined then to make up for every moment of neglect he had shown her.

From that day on, Connie began to read a Bible that someone had given her, and it wasn't long before she was regularly going to church. After a few weeks Jerry decided to go with her, just for moral support. It was an old, cold, brick Methodist church building that had a warm interior. The elderly minister and the people showed the Adamsons nothing but love and support. With Connie's gentle encouragement, Jerry was also able to curb his use of God's name in vain. This wasn't easy because it had rolled off his tongue for so many years, he didn't even know he was doing it.

Despite the fact that he was attending church, and despite his prayer after the house fire in England, Jerry still quietly leaned toward atheism, although for Connie's sake he never mentioned it. His thought was that we create a higher power, or a "God"—call it what you will—in times of crisis. With a cold objectivity, he remembered the circumstances in which he had prayed when his daughter had stopped breathing. The incident confirmed his belief: in his time of weakness he had called upon a greater power. This was a natural inclination for the human species. This was what was happening with Connie, and he hoped that her faith would help her through her ordeal.

Following one church meeting, Rev. Smalley and his wife invited the couple home for lunch. After the meal, the women chatted in the kitchen and Jerry and the reverend retired into the living room, something Jerry had hoped would happen. He wanted to test the man's faith, without hurting Connie's feelings or appearing rude.

As they sat on the soft lounge chairs, he picked up a cup of coffee, stirred it slowly and said, "Reverend, would you mind if I ask you a few questions about . . . about 'God,' and His existence? I consider myself a reasonably intelligent and well-read human being and tend to lean toward atheism, so I would like you to tell me why you have a belief in a Creator when there is so much evidence in the other direction."

Reverend Smalley smiled and said, "I would be happy to try to answer any questions, if you will stop calling me 'Reverend.' I'm Edwin."

"Sure," Jerry said. "Here's my question. I can understand why Connie suddenly wanted to go to church. Death is a very scary thing and that's when 'faith' comes in handy. My own father prayed when the Nazis were heading for Poland. I spent four years fighting with the French Resistance, and I would be a liar if I said that I never prayed when things were tough. But that's my point. When things get difficult, we all need to look to 'God' or the bottle—something to pull us through. I remember praying once and even being convinced that God answered my prayer, but I was backed into a corner and couldn't do anything but pray. I'm sure what I then thought was an answer to prayer was nothing but a coincidence."

With the minister patiently listening, Jerry continued. "Then there is actual evidence *against* the existence of God. First, there is the ever-present issue of suffering. If a God of love existed, He wouldn't allow it. What father would let his children starve to death, as we have seen happen in China in years past? Or what father would let his child suffer with cancer when he could easily cure her, as in the case of Connie?

"Second, what proof is there for His existence anyway? You can't see Him, hear Him, touch, taste, or smell Him. All I ever hear when it comes to God is, 'You've got to have faith.' Well, I'm sorry, Reverend…uh, Edwin…I don't want 'faith.' I want good, hard, concrete *evidence*."

Jerry sipped his coffee then set his cup to one side. "I must say I feel a bit uncomfortable," he said, shuffling in his seat. "Here I am a guest in your house, and I guess I have shaken your faith a little."

To his surprise, Edwin didn't look one bit shaken. He smiled politely and replied, "I had exactly the same sentiments for years. If I gave you a book, would you take the time to read it and get back to me with your thoughts? It's about atheists. It's called *God Doesn't Believe in Atheists*. If you take the ti—"

Jerry lifted his hand and interrupted, "I really don't think it will help."

The minister smiled in that he had uncovered the fact that Jerry wasn't asking questions at all, but merely airing his beliefs. "So, you are pretty sure of your facts?"

Jerry was quick to respond. "Sure? To be quite honest, I haven't begun to bring out all the other evidence to support atheism: the fact of evolution—you can't argue with science— the hypocrisy in the church, the hateful doctrine of Hell, and the fact that Hitler was a Christian."

Reverend Smalley leaned forward a little and said, "May I ask you a couple of questions?"

"Why not? Go ahead," Jerry retorted, confident that he could handle anything the minister had.

"Look around my house. Notice the windows, the door frames, the interior paneling, the wallpaper, the electrical wiring, the tiles on the roof, etc. If I asked you if there was a builder, what would you say to me?"

Jerry's expression revealed that he thought the question to be absurd and he said with a slight impatience, "The building *exists;* therefore there *must* be a builder. Buildings don't make themselves. I don't see your point."

"But you can't see him, hear him, touch, taste, or smell him. What actual *proof* is there that he exists?"

Jerry quietly said, "The *building.*"

"What then would you think of my mental capacity if I told you that there was no evidence that there was a builder? What would you think of my intellect if I said to you that I *really* believed that this house—with all the concrete, lumber, nails, glass, door frames, paneling, etc. —happened by pure chance, *by accident?*"

Suddenly, it seemed like a light switched on in Jerry's head. He thought for a moment and replied, "I would think you were a fool."

"Here's a second question. As an atheist, you believe that nothing created everything... a scientific impossibility?"

Jerry didn't answer.

"You can't truly believe that creation, or as a professing atheist you may call it Nature, made itself. This is because if it made itself, it had to pre-exist before it made itself to be able to have the ability to make itself. So, you are stuck with the scientific impossibility of believing that nothing created everything."

Jerry rubbed his chin thoughtfully. "No, I don't believe that. Obviously something created everything; I just don't believe that it was God, and particularly not the Christian God."

"So, Jerry, you're not an atheist. You are what's called an agnostic. You believe that there was or is some sort of creative force. But I want to take that a little further, if you will let me. I'm telling you something you already know intuitively. You know that creation is evidence of the Creator, because God gave you that knowledge. The book of Romans and Psalm 19 say that creation shouts to you of His genius, but you 'suppress' that knowledge because you know that it brings with it moral accountability. That God-given knowledge leaves you without excuse."

CHAPTER NINETEEN
THE NUMBER FORTY

∾∾

T HE CONVERSATION with Edwin shattered a lifetime of Jerry's philosophy. He couldn't argue with the simple fact that *everything* made had a maker. There wasn't a thing on the face of the earth that he could say didn't have some sort of maker, whether it was his car, his TV, his shoes, his telephone, his couch, or his house. All around him were flowers, birds, trees, and thousands of different animals—living things infinitely more complex than anything man had ever made.

He felt foolish that he had thought himself to be "intellectual" in his atheistic beliefs. He had also found an adequate answer to the next obvious question: Who made God? That one was reasonably simple. God has no beginning and no end. He is eternal. He dwells outside the dimension of "time" that He created.

A few days after this, at the insistence of his dying wife, Jerry agreed to pray what Connie called the "sinner's prayer," asking Jesus Christ to be his Lord and Savior. She said that all he needed was to really mean what he said, and from that time on he continued to attend church each Sunday until Connie's death.

∾◦∾

IT HAD BEEN three months since his beloved wife's passing. Jerry had shed a lot of tears. With their kids now grown, the house seemed very quiet and he had a lot of time alone to think.

Once again he sat in Edwin's home, but this time it was in the minister's study. The walls of the small room were lined with books—hundreds of books about God and the Bible. After a little small talk about such an impressive collection, Jerry said, "Edwin, I know I can be open with you. Since Connie died...well, even though I made a 'decision for Christ' some time ago, I seem to have lost faith in God. I was sincere when I prayed that sinner's prayer with Connie. She was deathly sick and so for her sake I really meant it, but to be honest nothing much happened. I kept going to church, and stopped cussing and drinking, but when I think about it, it was more out of respect for Connie than anything else.

"In fact, I haven't prayed in weeks," Jerry continued. "Not only that, I'm not sure of the Bible. Connie would read it all the time but I have no desire to. I feel bitter that God let her die. I wouldn't have bothered to come back and see you except that last night I had a dream I have had a number of times since the war. In it, a minister keeps pointing to me, out of all the people in the room, and accusing me of different things. I'm confused about what I'm supposed to do. One thing I do know—I can't go on as before, living in blind faith as though everything was all right."

"Oh, being a Christian isn't a matter of 'blind faith,'" Edwin replied with a gentle firmness in his voice. "The world thinks that's what is required, but it's not true.

"Seeing as you mentioned it, let's look at the Bible for a moment and see if you can be 'sure' of its authenticity. It was written over a period of 4,000 years by around forty different authors, from kings to fishermen, and yet there is incredible consistency throughout the whole of Scripture. Take for instance how God said in

Deuteronomy that if the Jews obeyed Him and kept His Law they would have His blessings of long life, health, and prosperity. However, if they disobeyed Him and became godless, giving themselves to idolatry which would lead to all types of sexual sin, greed, corruption, etc., He would allow them to be delivered into the hands of their enemies, so that, as a nation, they would be humbled and seek Him once again. This happened time and time again throughout the Old Testament, and has continued to happen right up until this present day.

"One interesting consistency is that the number forty is God's number of testing and deliverance. The Old Testament and the New Testament harmonize in this. God delivered Moses from Egypt when he was forty years old, then He waited forty years before He used Moses to deliver the Jewish people from Egypt. Moses was on the mountain with God for forty days and forty nights when he received the tablets of the Ten Commandments. God also tested the Jews in the wilderness for forty years before delivering them into the land of Canaan. Jesus was in the wilderness forty days while He was tempted by Satan, and He was seen on earth for forty days after His resurrection. This use of the number forty throughout Scripture attests to the fact that only God could have inspired such unerring consistency—and it's only one example of literally hundreds of perfect harmonies of numerical symmetry. That alone should convince an honest skeptic to at least set aside his doubts for a moment."

He paused his mini-sermon for a moment to smile at the thought of an "honest skeptic," because they were so few and far between, then added, "But there are also thousands of infallible prophecies which have been perfectly fulfilled, such as the Jews getting Jerusalem back, which happened in 1967, something God had promised thousands of years previous. There are also over three hundred prophecies related just to the coming of the Messiah, Jesus Christ. These fulfilled prophecies *prove* that the book was written by the only One who knows the future. And there is something else you need to hear."

Sitting up in his seat Jerry interjected, "At this point I don't doubt God's existence. What bothers me is the fact that I keep having this dream telling me I'm a sinner! I don't get it; I'm really not a bad person. I remember reading, in the book of Job I think, where he said that God terrified him with dreams. That's what's been happening with me. What does God want from me?"

"Jerry, you've been candid with me," said the old minister as he leaned forward in his chair, "so I trust you will let me be direct with you. Let me ask you a question. Have you obeyed the Ten Commandments?"

Jerry said with a shrug, "I have broken one or two... but who hasn't? What I am more concerned with is the fact that God allowed my wife to get cancer, *then He let her die*. Where's the justice in that?"

Edwin seemed to ignore that remark. "Well, let's look at the Ten Commandments, God's moral Law, for a moment and see how you do. How many lies do you think you have told in your whole life?"

In a flash Jerry thought of his childhood in Texas, his years in Germany and France, then the lies he told in England, and those he told to Connie when he was committing adultery. "Quite a few. But who hasn't lied? I think we are all guilty."

"What does that make you?" asked the minister. "What do you call someone who tells lies?"

"A sinner, I guess." The next statement made him shuffle in his seat.

"Yes, but more specifically...a *liar*," said Edwin. "Have you ever stolen something, even if it's small?"

Jerry admitted that he had.

"What does that make you?"

"A thief."

The reverend's eyes twinkled as he said, "No, it makes you a *lying* thief." He then looked at the Bible he had opened on his lap and read: "Ye have heard that it was said by them of old time, Thou shalt not commit adultery: But I say unto you, That whosever looketh on a wo-man to lust after her hath committed adultery with her already in his heart."

He seemed to look directly at Jerry with the same piercing gaze that Mr. von Ludendorff gave him in his nightmares, and asked, "Have you ever done that?"

Jerry tried to hide the fact that his mouth was dry and his heart was pounding in his chest. He rubbed his chin self-consciously and said, "Yes...once or twice."

The minister then looked even more intently at him and said, "Jerry, by your own admission, you are a lying, thieving, adulterer at heart, *and you have to face God on Judgment Day*... and we have only looked at three of the Ten Commandments. There are another seven you have to answer to, concerning blasphemy, greed, hatred, murder, honoring your parents, and giving to God what is rightly His in the area of worship, etc. On Judgment Day, if God was to judge you by the standard of His Law, do you think you would be innocent or guilty?"

He didn't hesitate to answer. "Guilty."

"Well, do you think you will go to Heaven or Hell?"

The answer was quick and positive: "Heaven!" Jerry said.

"Why? Is it because you think God is 'good' and therefore will overlook your sins?"

Jerry nodded in agreement with such an idea. He was pleased that Edwin had been able to articulate why he thought he should go to Heaven. His only hope was that God would understand his mistakes, but it seemed that the reverend didn't want to leave the conversation there.

"If a rapist and murderer expects a judge to overlook his crimes because he believes the judge is a 'good' man, he will probably hear him answer such a presumption by saying, 'You are right about one thing. I *am* a good man, and it is *because* of my goodness that I am going to see that you are punished and brought to justice.'

"Those who are hoping that God's goodness will overlook their sins will find that the very thing they are trusting in to save them will be the thing that will condemn them and send them to Hell."

Edwin then closed his Bible as if to rest his case. When he stood up and walked around his desk Jerry was thinking, *Don't leave me like this.* But he too rose to his feet and as they walked toward the door he asked the minister, "What do you think I should do?"

As they stood at the doorway he said, "Jerry, you know the gospel: that Jesus Christ, the Son of God, died to save us. You know that He bore the punishment for our sins. *We* broke the Law; *He* paid our fine. That means that God can now *legally* dismiss our case. He can commute our death sentence and let us live. You also know that Jesus rose from the dead. But you need to ask God to give you understanding about *what that means*, and you need to repent—turn from your sins—and put your faith in the Savior."

Then he paused as though he had thought of a better way to illustrate what he had just said.

"Jerry, it's like a man who found himself deeply in debt. He was *utterly* without hope. There was no way that he could pay his creditors. The law was about to take its fearful course, when a rich friend extended grace toward him and paid his debt in full. It was actually the law that *drove* him to grace. If the law hadn't pressured him, he wouldn't have sought help from his friend. Can you understand that?"

The old minister smiled gently, then quoted a hymn that he loved to sing: "'It was grace that taught my heart to fear, and grace my fears relieved.' Those are the words of a hymn the world sings—"Amazing Grace"—but it seems many have no understanding of what the words actually mean.

"When the Christian looks at the terrible price that the Law demanded—the suffering death of the Messiah—it horrifies him. Grace provided the payment, and it was at a terrible cost. The Bible puts it this way: 'Pass the time of your sojourning here in fear: forasmuch as ye know that ye were not redeemed with corruptible things, as silver and gold... but with the precious blood of Christ.'"

Jerry thought about the day the officers of the law drove him to Theodore's house and how

Grace welcomed him, and led him to Theodore who paid his debt in full. He *could* understand what the Bible was saying, more than the minister knew.

"Jerry, God's wrath abides upon every person who has transgressed His Commandments. If the Law is allowed to take its fearful course on the Day of Judgment, its sentence will be eternal Hell. It's the knowledge of our true state —that we are in *big* trouble—that drives us to the gospel of grace.

"Our salvation was no small thing. When Jesus suffered on the cross, He paid the fine with His own life's blood. Just as the friend showed that his love was more than mere lip service by paying the debt, so the cross is an evident expression of God's love and grace toward you and me. But these are just empty words until God reveals the truth of them to you."

Then Reverend Smalley reminded Jerry of the story of the Prodigal Son, a story he hadn't heard since his Sunday school days. Edwin refreshed his memory that it was the story Jesus told about a wayward son who left his father and ended up in a pigsty.

The young man took his inheritance and wasted it on immoral living, then returned penniless and asked for his father's forgiveness. As Edwin spoke of the rebellious son, Jerry quietly thought about *Johnny's* experience. Then, as he was beginning to walk away, he turned around and with a troubled expression asked, "What should I say to God?"

"Just pour out your heart to Him. It's like a man who has betrayed his wife's trust by committing adultery. His loving and faithful wife is more than willing to take him back, so in what attitude should he approach her, and what should he say to her?"

Jerry knew there was no way Edwin could have known about his affairs. He wrote off the first two stories, about the man who had all his debt paid and the son coming home destitute, as mere coincidence. But the third "illustration," about a husband who committed adultery, made him shudder. He *had* been unfaithful to his wife, but only he and the other women knew that.

Jerry said contritely, "His attitude should be one of genuine humility, humbled that his wife would take him back. He should simply say that he has violated her trust, that he has no words of justification for what he has done...and that he will never even *think* of committing adultery again."

"Go and do likewise," Edwin responded. "God isn't interested in your words, but in your heart. Repentance is telling God you are sorry for sinning against Him and you will never even *think* of doing it again. That husband may be tempted to lust after other women, but if he does, in light of the grace his wife showed him, he will immediately pull his thoughts back into line with his new resolve to do only what pleases her."

With that, he put one hand on Jerry's shoulder and prayed that God would continue to speak to him and bring him to a point of genuine repentance. Then he said, "If I were you, Jerry, I would go home, get on my knees, and read Psalm 51."

CHAPTER TWENTY
A SPECTACLE OF YOURSELF

∽◦∾

KEVIN KICKHAM was a good man. He smiled at Jerry and said, "I'm glad you came in. Some people put off getting a new prescription and end up doing permanent damage to their eyesight."

As Jerry's optometrist, he seemed to show a genuine concern for his welfare. What he said made Jerry feel pleased that he had taken the time out of his busy schedule to have his eyes checked.

After the exam, he was ushered into a waiting room and told that he would have the new glasses in his hands within the hour.

As he took a seat, he scanned the room and noticed three other people. Sitting next to each other were a very large woman and a very large boy who stared back at him. They were apparently mother and son. A few seats down sat a woman whose face was hidden by a magazine she was holding a couple of inches from her nose. *No doubt she's waiting for her new prescription*, Jerry thought.

He looked beside him at the mound of magazines and a small stack of bright yellow bookmarks carrying the name, address, and phone number of the optometrist. Across the top was boldly written "What could be more important than your eyes?"

He picked up a *Time* magazine and flicked through it. It was two weeks old, and Jerry was intimately familiar with almost every news item in it. He put it down, picked up a bookmark and read the words again: "What could be more important than your eyes?"

I would hate to be blind, he thought. *Imagine seeing nothing but darkness until the day you die. I wouldn't give up my eyes for the world.*

He slipped the bookmark into his coat pocket, then picked up another magazine, set it on his lap, and for some reason began to think about Connie. It was strange that he didn't realize how much he loved her until she got cancer. Again the nagging began in his mind: *Why? Why did God let her die? She was a good woman. She was a faithful wife. She believed in God and look what He did to her!*

Then he thought about the conversation he had had with the minister the previous day. He went home that night and read Psalm 51 in Connie's Bible. It was just a prayer that King David prayed after he committed adultery. After reading it, Jerry decided that he would try to clean up his act, especially after hearing what the Bible said about "lust." He knew that it was wrong to let pornographic thoughts invade his mind, so he would try to think *pure* thoughts.

At the very moment he thought that, the woman opposite him lowered the magazine from in front of her face. Jerry had imagined her to be a little homely looking with thick glasses. *She wasn't.* In fact, she was gorgeous. She was so stunning that he found himself wanting to stare at her. At that moment, she crossed her legs—what he noticed were very shapely legs. He quickly picked up the magazine and thought, *Wonderful! I decide not to lust after women, and immediately I do it.*

He didn't feel he had gotten a good look at her, so he discreetly peeped over the top of the magazine, but to his horror she glanced at him at that same instant. He put the magazine back on his lap and began to casually flick through it. He hadn't realized that he had grabbed a woman's publication, and almost every page had pictures of *more* ravishing women—usually advertising lingerie.

A battle began to rage in his mind: "This is ridiculous! There's nothing wrong with just *looking* at beautiful women. *But would I want other men 'looking' at my sister like I look at other men's sisters?* It's not *hurting* anyone! *Maybe not, but God says lust is adultery.* Well, why hasn't this sort of thing bothered me before? *Because you've never tried to stop before, that's why.* It's only natural for a man to sexually desire a woman. *Yes, it does come naturally, but you know that pornography is wrong in God's sight, so why would you think He condones pornography of the mind?*"

Jerry put the magazine back and tried to pull his thoughts together. It was as though his conscience, which had been dead for so long, had suddenly sprung to life.

He felt annoyed that something he enjoyed was threatened with being taken from him by puritanical fanaticism. He was fine until that stupid minister pushed the Ten Commandments down his throat. He decided he would forget about the talk with Edwin and merely try to live a good life.

As he drove home that day he wore his new glasses. They didn't help him much. *Dr. Kickham had done a fine job*—all they did was bring into sharper focus *how much* he lusted after women. He had never been so conscious of the fact that he desired almost every female his lustful eyes could find.

When he arrived home he felt like he had been wallowing in a pigsty of his own sinful desires. His time at the optometrist's had truly been eye-opening.

∽◌∾

"EDWIN, THIS IS going to sound a little strange." Jerry gave a small nervous laugh. "I have been thinking about the last time we spoke, and I have come to the conclusion that I don't have any 'faith' in God. Don't get me wrong—I believe in His existence, but...*I really don't know what I'm trying to say...*"

It had been three days since Jerry's visit to the eye doctor—three long days of an awareness of a sense of guilt, to a point where he felt he couldn't face God in prayer.

"I'm sorry to call you at dinner time, but this is *really* starting to bother me."

Edwin assured him that he was pleased to hear from him *any* time of the day or night. "Jerry, there are different *types* of faith," he explained. "In the past you denied God's existence, then you became aware of Him as a Creator, yet all that time *He* has been intimately aware of you, despite your lack of faith in Him. For example, even the hairs of your head are numbered. He knows when you sit down and rise up, and He's acquainted with *all* your ways. In fact, there is not a word on your tongue that He doesn't know altogether. Before you were formed in the womb, He knew you. You are not just some evolutionary accident without rhyme or reason.

"After you left, I did a quick study of the meaning of your name, which has real significance. It shows how God's hand is upon every one of us. This is what my book of names and their meanings said: Jeremiah Adamson—*Jehovah will exalt, son of Adam.*

"God may have even used you for His purposes in the past without you having the slightest awareness of it. No, Jeremiah, your lack of faith doesn't make any difference to the faithfulness of God..."

Jerry interrupted, "When I made my 'decision,' I had some sort of faith. I really tried to believe that God would heal Connie, but that became overwhelmed with anger and bitterness when she grew worse. Now there's just nothing there."

"Jerry, the 'faith' the Bible speaks of regarding salvation is more than an intellectual resolution. It's not merely a matter of asking Jesus Christ into your heart, but what the Bible calls 'repentance toward God and faith toward our Lord Jesus Christ.'

"Jesus warned that many would seek to enter into the kingdom of God and 'would not be able.' He said to *strive* to enter the straight gate; that means to *agonize* to get in."

"I appreciate what you're saying," Jerry replied, "but I *still* feel confused, and I still have this anger about Connie's death."

"That will go away in time. Jerry, I don't profess to have all the answers or to know the mind of God, but one thing I have seen again and again is that suffering has a way of humbling the proud human heart. The prophet Jeremiah said of the Jews who suffered, 'The people which were left of the sword found grace in the wilderness.' Sometimes the only prayer we offer our

Creator is 'Why?' The wilderness of life and the sword of tribulation can bring us to our knees. It looks like God's hand is on you, Jerry."

CHAPTER TWENTY-ONE
THE ENEMY OF GOD

∞∞∞

LATER THAT NIGHT Jerry went to the bookshelf and pulled out Connie's King James Bible. The pages were worn for a book that was just a few months old, and hundreds of verses were underlined with notes written beside them.

He found the book of Psalms and opened it again to Psalm 51.

Connie had neatly printed in the margin beside verse 4, "See James 4:4," so he looked in the index and turned to the verse in the book of James. It seemed to jump off the page at him: "Ye adulterers and adulteresses, know ye not that the friendship of the world is enmity with God? whosoever therefore will be a friend of the world is the enemy of God."

This time Connie had written another note beside it: "You were 'enemies in your mind by wicked works' (Colossians 1:21)—natural mind 'enmity' to God. See also Matthew 5:28,29."

Jerry turned to the verses to see what they were. His heart skipped a beat as he read the same verse that Edwin had read to him, about lust being adultery of the heart. It wasn't marked by Connie so he thought, *I must try to remember where this is.* It was then that he recalled the bookmark he had picked up in the eye doctor's waiting room. He got it from his coat pocket, but as he went to place it in the Bible, his eyes fell on the next verse: "And if thy right eye offend thee, pluck it out, and cast it from thee: for it is profitable for thee that one of thy members perish, and not that thy whole body should be cast into hell."

He stared again at the heading on the yellow bookmark: "What could be more important than your eyes?" and thought, *Nothing could be more important, except the eternal salvation of my soul.*

He slowly turned back again to Psalm 51. It began by making reference to King David's adultery: "A Psalm of David, when Nathan the prophet came unto him, after he had gone in to Bathsheba." In the margin of the Bible he found more neat handwriting, "See 2 Samuel 12," so to get a background on the incident he turned there and began to read.

It was the story of King David and how he lusted after a beautiful woman named Bathsheba as he spied her bathing. He found out she was married, yet he committed adultery with her, had her husband killed, and then married her.

God then sent the prophet Nathan to reprove him. The man of God told David a parable about something that, as a former shepherd, he could understand: sheep. Nathan told a story about a rich man who, rather than take from his own flock, killed a poor man's pet lamb to feed a stranger.

David was indignant and said that the guilty party would die for his crime. Nathan then exposed the king's sin of taking another man's "lamb," saying, "Thou art the man . . . Wherefore hast thou despised the commandment of the LORD, to do evil in his sight?" When David showed signs of sorrow, Nathan then said, "The LORD also hath put away thou sin; thou shalt not die."

Jerry then turned back to Psalm 51 and wondered what David's attitude would be when he approached God after his sin was exposed. He slowly read out loud the following words: "Have mercy upon me, O God, according to thy lov-ingkindness: according unto the multitude of thy tender mercies blot out my transgressions. Wash me thoroughly from mine iniquity, and cleanse me from my sin. For I acknowledge my transgressions: and my sin is ever before me. Against thee, thee only, have I sinned, and done this evil in thy sight."

It was at those words that he stopped. They were no longer the expressions of a sinful king of Israel, but they were coming from Jerry's own heart: "Against thee, thee only, have I sinned."

He dropped to his knees as a flood of his own immorality flashed through his mind. He remembered hating people during the war, just because of their nationality. He recalled all the people he had wronged in business. He began to think of how many of the Ten Commandments he had broken. He hadn't merely coveted things that belonged to other people, he had stolen many times over his lifetime. He thought of the lust that had burned in his heart, his incessant lies, the hatred and bitterness, his ingratitude for the gift of life, his proud atheistic arrogance, and his self-righteousness. He thought of the wrong that he had done to Connie by committing adultery, not once, but many times through his one-night stands. A sense of shame enveloped him and he began to sigh deeply and weep like a little child. It seemed that there was a massive weight pressing on his chest. He couldn't lift his head, but stammered, "God, I have sinned against You! I deserve to go to Hell. Please forgive me."

As he did so, the weight lifted from his chest, and at the same time it was as though a dark cloud lifted from his tormented mind. From the time he was a child, he had heard that Jesus Christ died on the cross for the sins of the world, but suddenly it dawned on him that when Jesus was on the cross so long ago, He was suffering for the sins of Jeremiah P. Adamson. He had never seen the cross as an expression of God's love *for him* before! He realized, *This was God in human form taking the punishment due to me!* The words of Edwin came back to him: Jerry had broken God's Law, but because Jesus had paid the fine for him he was free to leave the courtroom.

His eyes fell on verse 10 of the Bible that lay open in front of him. Through tears he read its words as his own prayer: "Create in me a clean heart, O God; and renew a right spirit within me."

He sighed again deeply. Words couldn't describe the peace that flooded his mind. God loved him despite his sin, had forgiven him *because of the cross*, and Jesus Christ through the power of His eternal Spirit had made His residence in him, granting him everlasting life.

∞

WHEN JERRY awoke the following morning, he wondered if what had happened to him the night before was another one of his weird dreams that involved God. Suddenly, he realized that the reason for Connie's suffering didn't matter anymore! *That was in God's hands.* One day he would understand why it happened. "*I have faith*," he said smiling. "I have faith in God! I trust Him."

As he walked into the living room with his cup of coffee, he noticed that he had left the Bible lying out from the night before. When he went to place it back on the shelf, he saw an old book the minister had given Connie. It was about the life of John Wesley, the founder of the Methodist church.

Out of curiosity, he picked up the book and thumbed through it. He began reading the words of the great preacher at the bottom of a page:

It remains only to show, in the fourth and last place, the use of the Law... Some there are whose hearts have been broken in pieces in a moment, either in sickness or in health, without any visible cause, or any outward means whatever; and others (one in an age) have been awakened to a sense of the "wrath of God abiding on them," by hearing that "God was in Christ, reconciling the world unto himself." But it is the ordinary method of the Spirit of God to convict sinners by the Law. It is this which, being set home on the conscience, generally breaketh the rocks in pieces. It is more especially this part of the Word of God which is quick and powerful, full of life and energy, "and sharper than any two-edged sword." This, in the hand of God and of those whom he hath sent, pierces through all the folds of a deceitful heart and "divides asunder even the soul and the spirit;" yea, as it were, the very "joints and marrow." By this is the sinner discovered to himself. All his fig-leaves are torn away, and he sees that he is "wretched, and poor, and miserable, and blind, and naked." The Law flashes conviction on every side. He feels himself a mere sinner. He has nothing to pay. His "mouth is stopped," and he stands "guilty before God."

To slay the sinner is then, the first use of the Law; to destroy the life and strength wherein he trusts, and convince him that he is dead while he liveth; not only under the sentence of death, but actually dead unto God, void of all spiritual life, "dead in trespasses and sins." The second use of it is to bring him unto life, unto Christ that he may live. It is true, in performing both these offices, it acts the part of a severe schoolmaster. It drives us by force, rather than draws us by love. And yet love is the spring of all. It is the spirit of love which, by this painful means, tears away our confidence in the flesh, which leaves us no broken reed whereon to trust, and so constrains the sinner, stripped of all to cry out in the bitterness of his soul or groan in the depth of his heart, I give up every plea beside, Lord, I am damned; but thou hast died.

Jerry was wide-eyed as he read Wesley's words. He whispered, "That's why I didn't see my need for Jesus Christ for so long. I didn't have the knowledge of the Law and therefore didn't understand my guilt—that I had sinned against God!"

Later that morning, a letter arrived from the State Department. It was an official dispatch saying that they had recently received a bag of mail containing two thousand letters. The German government informed them that it had been buried beneath the rubble in the basement of a condemned building, which apparently had been a temporary post office in Berlin during the war.

Within the large envelope was a smaller envelope, one that was addressed to Jerry in his sister's handwriting. On it was an official-looking Red Cross stamp postmarked August 9, 1944.

As he carefully opened the letter from his precious, long-lost sister, his hands trembled with emotion. Oh, how it wrenched at his heart to see that familiar handwriting, the blue ink now faded to a reddish brown. He closed his eyes tightly for a few seconds to clear them of tears so he could focus. He read:

August 7, 1944

Dearest Jerry, How I miss seeing your face. I pray that you are well and that God's hand is upon you. I am not able to give many details, but shortly after I was arrested, I was sent to the flea-infested Ravensbrück labor camp along with about 400 other women. I befriended two Jewish sisters who invited me to a Bible study. What great light we have found in this dark place!

I saw Grandmother in Ravensbrück when I first arrived, but then she disappeared. I fear the worst.

May you find what I have found in this place, and may God keep you in His caring arms.

Your loving sister, Lillian
P.S. Colossians 1:26,27

Jerry stared at the postscript, which seemed to jump out at him. He turned to those verses in the Bible and read them out loud: "Even the mystery which hath been hid from ages and from generations, but now is made manifest to his saints: to whom God would make known what is the riches of the glory of this mystery among the Gentiles; which is Christ in you, the hope of glory…"

Tears welled in his eyes. He had to blink to clear them as he read the verses again: "this mystery…Christ in you, the hope of glory." He could almost see Mr. von Ludendorff smiling at the thought that the sentence he had begun about forty years ago had finally been completed. The "mystery" was the miracle of the Author and the source of all life dwelling in him. This is an enigma to a spiritually blind world. God is life. He is not separate from life, He is life, and when He makes His dwelling place within a mortal human being, that person becomes immortal. He receives eternal life and is "sealed" with the Holy Spirit.

Jerry now understood the meaning of Jesus' death on the cross and its legal implications. God was a Judge, while Jerry was a guilty criminal who was guilty of violating the moral Law. He was heading for a prison, a place called Hell, without parole. But Jesus had stepped into the courtroom 2,000 years ago and paid Jerry's fine in full through His suffering death and resurrection. When He cried out, "It is finished!" on the cross, He was saying, "The debt has been paid!" The demands of eternal justice had been satisfied. That meant that Jerry's case could be dismissed. The Judge could legally commute his death sentence and let him live forever. This was the mystery that Connie had tried to explain. It was the mystery that Reverend Smalley began to uncover for him. It had been there all the time but he couldn't see it until God had given him light.

With his hands shaking with excitement, he turned to the front of his Bible and wrote the words: "Today, May 14, 1978, I discovered 'the mystery, which was kept secret since the world be—.' He stopped and stared at the date he had just written. Tears began to fall onto the open pages of the Bible in front of him: May 14! That was a day he vowed he would never forget. It was the date he had visited the church, May 14, 1938. Exactly forty years ago! It was God's number of deliverance—forty years *to the very day* since he first sat in the Bible study and heard Mr. von Ludendorff ask, "Do you know the mystery of Christ?"

∞∞

AS WAS HIS HABIT, Jerry watched the news on television that night. He listened to the concerned anchorman speak of the rise in anti-

Semitism in the United States. He watched a debate on the virtues of "mercy killings," of the possibilities of future experimentation with fetal tissue, on the rights of women to choose to take the life of their unborn children through abortion.

Some time later, he listened to a doctor concerned about the increase of parental abuse of children. The man supported the licensing of people to *be* parents. "After all," he said, "we have marriage licenses; we require licenses to drive cars, to own guns, to fish, to own a dog. Isn't parenting a more important issue?

"If the parents don't raise their children in a way that is consistent with the standards of the U.S., then the parents should not have the privilege of raising children. The state should remove them."

What scared Jerry was that it *sounded* reasonable.

That evening he began to understand that the war he fought in Europe was a minor skirmish compared to the *real* war. There was another war—a battle between man and his Creator, between the devil and God, between wrong and right.

There were, in truth, two wars. One was man fighting man, and the other, man fighting God. But Jerry had laid down his arms. He had relinquished his weapons of rebellion and enlisted on the winning side, in the war that would end all wars—the "good fight of faith." He had come to the end of a long journey and begun another one that would lead him to a "far more exceeding and eternal weight of glory." Jeremiah P. Adamson had found the glory that would *never* fade: the mystery of Christ in him, "the hope of glory."

Later that night, he reflected on how many times he could have been killed during the war. He thought deeply about the night of the fire, and how he might have died, had not his faithful canine friend broken free from his rope and awakened him from a deep sleep.

He bowed solemnly before his Creator and prayed: "Dear God, let me be as a faithful friend, who will break free from the restraints of fear, and awaken those who are sleeping in darkness, indifferent to the 'fire of Your wrath.' Let me sound the alarm, and cry, *'Awake thou that sleepest, and arise from the dead, and Christ shall give thee light!'*

"Deliver them, dear Lord...deliver them that they too would come to know You, and find eternal life.

"Bring them out of darkness into the glorious light of the gospel of Christ, who is the image of God. Let Your face shine upon them and reveal to them the enigma of immortality, *'the mystery, which was kept secret since the world began.'*"

This book is available in bulk at a very low cost. Please, consider purchasing copies and giving them away. Call 800-437-1893 for details or see www.LivingWaters.com.

RESOURCES

If you have not yet placed your trust in Jesus Christ and would like additional information, please visit LivingWaters.com and check out the following helpful resources:

The Evidence Study Bible. Answers to over 200 questions, thousands of comments, and over 130 informative articles will help you better comprehend the Christian faith.

How to Know God Exists: Scientific Proof of God. Clear evidences for His existence will convince you that belief in God is reasonable and rational—a matter of fact and not faith.

Why Christianity? (DVD). If you have ever asked what happens after we die, if there is a Heaven, or how good we have to be to go there, this DVD will help you.

If you are a new believer, please read *Save Yourself Some Pain*, written just for you (available free online at LivingWaters.com, or as a booklet).

For Christians

Please visit our website where you can sign up for our free weekly e-newsletter. To learn how to share your faith the way Jesus did, don't miss these helpful resources:

God Has a Wonderful Plan for Your Life: The Myth of the Modern Message (our most important book). This essential teaching, in a brief, easy-to-read book, is designed for anyone who wants to quickly learn how to share the gospel biblically.

Hell's Best Kept Secret and *True & False Conversion.* Listen to these vital messages free at LivingWaters.com.

How to Bring Your Children to Christ … & Keep Them There. These time-tested principles will help you guide your children to experience genuine salvation and avoid the pitfall of rebellion.

You can also gain further insights by watching the *Way of the Master* television program (WayoftheMaster.com) or listening to the Living Waters podcast.

For a catalog of Ray Comfort's resources, visit LivingWaters.com, call 800-437-1893, or write to: Living Waters Publications, P.O. Box 1172, Bellflower, CA 90707.